THIS IS NOT A LOVE SONG

ALSO BY BRENDAN MATHEWS

The World of Tomorrow

THIS IS NOT A LOVE SONG

STORIES

BRENDAN MATHEWS

Little, Brown and Company
New York Boston London

Compilation copyright © 2019 Brendan Mathews

Little, Brown and Company
Hachette Book Group
1290 Avenue of the Americas, New York, NY 10104
littlebrown.com

First Edition: February 2019

Little, Brown and Company is a division of Hachette Book Group, Inc. The Little, Brown name and logo are trademarks of Hachette Book Group, Inc.

These stories originally appeared, sometimes in different form, in the following publications: "My Last Attempt to Explain to You What Happened with the Lion Tamer" in *Cincinnati Review* and *Port Magazine* (UK); "Airborne" in *Epoch;* "Salvage" in *FiveChapters;* "How Long Does the First Part Last?" in *Glimmer Train;* "The Drive" in *Hobart;* "Henry and His Brother" in *Manchester Review* (UK); "Look at Everything" (as "What We Make") in *Southern Review;* "Heroes of the Revolution" in *TriQuarterly;* "Dunn & Sons" and "This Is Not a Love Song" in *Virginia Quarterly Review.* "My Last Attempt to Explain to You What Happened with the Lion Tamer" and "This Is Not a Love Song" were reprinted in *The Best American Short Stories* in 2010 and 2014, respectively.

ISBN 978-0-316-38214-4
LCCN 2018952129

10 9 8 7 6 5 4 3 2 1

LSC-C

Printed in the United States of America

To Nora, Fiona, Cormac, and Greta,
whose stories are still in progress

Contents

THIS IS NOT A LOVE SONG

Heroes of the Revolution

Is nice!" Vitas said. "Is really very nice!"

"She's awful. A monster." Edina kicked an apple out of the narrow path and into the low-slung branches of a tree. The trees were small and spidery, each one a spray of branches erupting from a knobby trunk.

"Monster?" he said. "No! Kirsten is sweet girl."

"She asks too many questions," Edina said. " 'What did you do last night?' 'What kind of music do you listen to?' 'Where did you get those shoes? Are they Bosnian? Do they make shoes in Bosnia?' "

"You are reporter," he said, his voice sly, teasing. "You are all the time asking questions."

"But why does she need to know these things? Am I the president? A general? A war criminal?" Edina and Vitas had been tromping through the orchard for almost an hour. It was late in the season and the ground was littered with fallen apples, their burnt-orange flesh dissolving at the slightest pressure. "There is no reason," she said. "She just wants to know."

"Is making friends," Vitas said. "You know how is making friends? Ask questions, answer questions, talk about somethings."

Edina shook her head. "She doesn't care. She thinks if she listens to me, then I have to listen when it's her turn to talk."

"Is not so wicked," he said. "Is nice, nice girl."

Edina had a catalog of reasons why Kirsten was not, in fact, a nice, nice girl, but before she could cite these for Vitas she squashed an apple with her foot. She was wearing low heels, a long coat, and a black pantsuit; entirely the wrong outfit for apple-picking. Edina blamed Kirsten for all of it: for her cold, sore feet; for the mud on the nicest pair of slacks that she'd brought to the States; for the smell of rotting apples that packed her head like wet wool.

It couldn't have taken her more than half a minute to wipe the apple mush off her shoe, but when she looked up, she was alone. She spoke Vitas's name quietly at first, then called out, unable to suppress the edge in her voice. It was only ten meters to the end of the row, but she stumbled on the stiff tufts of yellowed grass and snagged her coat on the spindly branches. Jerking her arm out of the tree's grip, she lost her balance and leaned into the trees on the other side of the path. All around her, branches raked her face and threatened to pull her down. "Vitas!"

She heard him answer from the end of the lane, his voice rising over the tangle of tree limbs and rotten fruit. "Edina! Where you are?"

She was far from home, in the middle of an orchard, in a lane of stunted trees that grew dense as a hedgerow. Edina focused on his voice, not on the way she lurched into the trees on either side of her. Sliding on the wet grass, her hands batting at the branches, she bolted from the path, emerging into the wide, tire-rutted lane that bisected the orchard.

"There you are," he said, his face blooming into a smile. "Come see." He beckoned her with a tilt of his head, but before she drew closer he opened his cupped palms. "Is Jewish apple."

Edina tried to catch her breath. She ran one hand over her head, checking for the silver clip that gathered her hair at the nape of her neck. She felt a fine haze of stiff, unruly grays rising off her scalp, refusing to be patted back in place. A swath of hair hung limply across her forehead.

"Gravenstein," he said, slowly working the syllables. He pointed to a white sign painted with shaky black letters. Similar signs marked each row in the orchard: JONATHAN, CORTLAND, ENGLISH SWEET, PINK LADY. Vitas plucked another apple, its skin mottled red and yellow, and rotated it in his palm.

"You would like?" he said, extending his hand with a flourish.

"No," she said, gulping the sodden air. The day was spongy and damp—Midwestern autumn hinting at the early arrival of winter. "No more apples." She was bent over, trying to catch her breath, but when she saw Vitas's face—his broad grin warping into puzzlement, even concern—she forced a smile. "Don't you know?" she said. "It's bad luck to pick Jewish apples on the Sabbath."

Vitas laughed his big booming laugh, his head thrown back, the hinge of his jaw springing open. Edina needed to find a word for that kind of laughter in her dictionary: *chortle, cackle, guffaw.*

"Are afraid you will be striked with lightning bolt?" he said. "Or pillar of fires?"

"If God could start a nice, warm fire, I might start believing in Him." She folded her arms across her chest, one hand clutching the lapels of her coat.

"If God will not save you, then this will." Vitas drew a large flask from inside his coat.

"If there's slivovitz in there I'm going to kiss you on the mouth."

"And where you kiss me if is vodka?"

Vitas was much better at this—this delicate business of sparking interest and feeding it by breath and movement until it took on a blazing life of its own. She wanted to tell herself that she was simply out of practice, but she knew that even when she had been young and eager, the perfect thing to say didn't come to her until hours after it was needed, when she was alone in her apartment, scribbling overheated stanzas in her notebook.

Vitas had caught her off guard; in recent years, she seemed to find herself across the table only from the bookish ones— bespectacled, library-pale, with matted hair and only the most casual acquaintance with hygiene—wondering how much time had to pass before she could say *Thanks, oh, don't bother, good night.* Vitas was a different type altogether. A big, bushy-headed blond with eyes like frozen lakes and a nose like a hawk's beak, he looked more like a Viking prince than a Slavic monk. She didn't know if there were Vikings in Lithuania, but she was willing to believe that centuries ago a shaggy berserker with horns on his helmet and an absurd sense of humor had crossed the Baltic, retired from pillaging, and put down roots in Vilnius.

The same fellowship that had brought Vitas from Lithuania to Chicago had brought Edina from Bosnia and half a dozen other journalists from India, Brazil, Mexico, and South Africa. For two months she had listened to Vitas's laughter echoing in the halls as he cajoled the others into joining him for drinks after work. She had always turned down the offers; she didn't like crowds, she would say, or she had work to do. The journalism fellowship was only three months long, and her agenda didn't include much time for socializing, and certainly none for nurturing a crush on one of the other visiting fellows.

She took the flask, cold to the touch, and tilted it back for a quick nip, then again for a stinging throatful of liquor. The mouth of the flask tasted like cigarettes and something hard and sharp. Slate. Or iron.

"God," she said, her voice hoarse, "that does help."

"Is one thing we can thank Russians for," he said. "Maybe is only thing." He raised the flask in salute, said a quick *Sveikata,* and took a drink.

She held out her hand for the flask, and as Vitas's eyes blazed with approval, she mentally rifled through the scanty file of Vitas-related facts and observations she had compiled. He was around her age, perhaps a little older, closing in on fifty. He worked for a newspaper in Vilnius and was writing a series of articles on ties between organized crime in Chicago and Lithuania's booming black market. He dressed far better than any reporter she knew; his apple-picking outfit consisted of a buttery suede coat, plush wide-wale corduroys, and Italian-made boots—proof, perhaps, that his interest in black-market goods wasn't purely professional. And now this latest bit of information: he was showing an interest in Edina that she considered far more than collegial.

She wasn't sure what had changed between them, but it had started the moment Vitas had signaled, with a furtive wave, to turn into a lane marked GOLDEN DELICIOUS. Maybe it was because he was handsome, although Edina wanted to believe that it took more than that. Maybe it was because he didn't ask much of her, just joked and offered small observations, and that was enough to make an afternoon in the orchard bearable. Or maybe it was because she was far from home and couldn't resist the urge, like so many others who had come to this country, to shake loose from her past, if only for a few hours.

Edina was getting ahead of herself. He was only being friendly; Vitas was nothing if not friendly. And it was nice, after all, just wandering together in the orchard, even if her ears stung from the cold and her toes felt stiff and frail as matchsticks. Vitas's flask kept the cloying scent at bay and was probably the source of those thoughts about how warm it must be where his arm met his shoulder. She could close her eyes and allow herself to lean into that spot; it was that easy. Except she wasn't sure what he would do next, and was even less sure of what she would do.

"YOO-HOO! YOO-HOO!" Edina and Vitas stopped in a row of Granny Smiths, listening to the looping, birdlike call. They exchanged a brief look before Edina lowered her eyes and sighed.

"She hasn't seen us yet," Edina said. "We still have time to escape."

"Is too late," he said, pointing up the lane. "She sees us."

Kirsten was striding toward them, waving and *yoo-hoo*ing the whole way. She had graduated the previous spring with a degree in something called American Studies and was working at the university while she applied to graduate school. One of her duties was showing the visiting journalists what she called "the real America." In the first two months, they had roasted in the sun-scorched bleachers at a Cubs game, been packed into a blues bar next to a table full of screeching bachelorette-party-goers, and had endured a lurching boat tour of the city's skyline. Today's outing was supposed to be a walking tour of the Frank Lloyd Wright houses in Oak Park, but at some point during Friday night's after-work happy hour—which Edina had not attended—Kirsten had decided that a day in the orchard would be more fun. As American as apple pie, she had said, and although the plan had changed, no one informed Edina until the next morning, after she had folded herself into the tiny backseat of Kirsten's sports coupe.

Kirsten, however, had dressed for the occasion. She wore a puffy orange vest that reminded Edina of a life jacket; a snug, cabled turtleneck; blue jeans that fit like a second skin; and a fleecy muffler and matching cap that Edina suspected cost more than her entire fellowship stipend. Kirsten's outfit, so perfect for a day in the country, brought the frigid sting back to Edina's feet. She burrowed her hands deeper into the tatty satin lining of her pockets, wishing she had something she could throw at Kirsten.

"There you are!" Kirsten said as Vitas and Edina drew closer. "I was going to organize a search party!" Kirsten explained that the rest of the visiting fellows had left the orchard half an hour ago—news that made Edina regret, in some way, the time spent walking with Vitas.

"Where are all your apples?" Kirsten said, looking from Vitas to Edina. Edina shrugged.

"You guys!" Kirsten said, her voice mixing delight and disapproval. "Apple-picking is about picking apples." Her bag bulged at the sides; apples were piled precariously over the lip.

"Is why we have none," Vitas said. "You pick them all."

"You're going to make me wonder what you two were up to out there," Kirsten said. "All that time alone and you didn't pick any apples?"

"I pick one," Vitas said, holding up the Gravenstein.

"That still leaves a lot of time—"

"So, we are finished?" Edina said. She didn't want Kirsten insinuating anything. What she wanted from Kirsten was silence and a ride. Over the tops of the trees she could see the roof of the barn that stood next to the parking lot. If they left now, they could be back in Evanston by five; time enough for a hot shower before dinner with Vitas—assuming he was free, assuming he was interested.

"We're done with the apple-picking," Kirsten said, "but now comes the best part."

"Better than this?" Vitas said. He spread his arms wide, as if to embrace every tree in the orchard. "Is not possible!"

"Vitas, you are so *mean*." Kirsten gave one of his hands a

playful shove, and like a mechanical toy, Vitas windmilled his arm, snatched the hat from her head, and ran down the lane, the hat held high. Kirsten shrieked and chased him, leaving Edina alone with the bag of apples. Up the lane, Vitas stopped and held the hat above Kirsten, daring her to jump up and grab it. Kirsten raised her hands like a ballerina, her sweater riding up to expose a swath of her taut golden belly. Kirsten's body advertised the nation's technological superiority in gymnasium equipment, and her hair flowed glossy and viscous as an oil spill. Edina could see the smile erupt on Vitas's face from thirty feet away. After a few more feints, he returned the hat to her and they walked side by side toward the barn. Kirsten lurched into Vitas as if trying to knock him down. As she thudded harmlessly against his side, he wrapped his arm across her shoulders and pulled her closer. Their laughter sparkled in the leaden air.

THE OLD BARN had been converted into a gift shop and a café, where families in flannel shirts and cartoon-bright synthetic pullovers huddled around tables dense with cups of coffee and cider. The walls were decorated with daguerreotypes of stunned-looking men with stiff beards and stern, pinch-faced women in black dresses—pioneers who had settled the American Midwest but seemed uncertain about whether the years of plowing, rail-splitting, and Indian-killing had been worth the effort. When Edina entered, Kirsten and Vitas were in line at the bakery counter, still laughing over some shared joke. Edina blew into her hands and staggered, as if the floor were also shivering, toward the potbellied stove in one corner.

She intercepted Vitas as he ferried cups of cider to a booth in the back of the room. "So, you and Kirsten," she said. "You are bosom buddies?"

"I tell you: is nice girl." He raised his hands in protest, or mock surrender, nearly spilling the cider. "Is true!"

"Oh, she's very nice. She has many fine . . . attributes," Edina said, her hands cupped in front of her chest. She had meant it to sound lighthearted, but the words left a bitter taste in her mouth.

Vitas winced and then mimicked Kirsten's heady squeal: "You are so *mean!*"

He set the cups on a table fashioned from heavily varnished pine planks. Years of apple-pickers had gouged the surface with names, dates, and declarations of love. Edina and Vitas slid into opposite sides of the booth, and amid the unzippings and unbuttonings that came with getting settled, Kirsten appeared.

"Ta-da!" she said, maneuvering an aluminum dish to the center of the table. "I couldn't let you go home without having a slice of apple pie." Edina stared at the lattice of sugared pastry laid like fingers over the congealed pie filling. She had been ravenous when they entered the café, but when she saw the pie, hunger gave way to nausea.

"You have got to try this," Kirsten said, pushing a paper plate toward Edina. "You'll love it." Whatever smell of cinnamon or caramelized sugar had emanated from the pie when it was fresh from the oven had long since dissipated. Edina pictured the bakers combing the orchard for apples, finding a few that were barely ripe, then rounding out the recipe with whatever they could find on the ground. Kirsten drew a line through the center with a short plastic knife and began sawing at the scalloped crust.

"Perhaps later." Edina swallowed hard. She saw Kirsten steal a look at Vitas.

"Come on," she said, her voice the singsong lilt that adults used with reluctant children. "You'll love it."

Edina extracted a pea-size morsel from the crust—more a biopsy than a bite. She examined it, noting the grit of the sugar, before popping it into her mouth. Kirsten's eyes were wide, expectant.

"It's good," Edina said. She knew that she was being too sour, too obviously displeased with the whole idea of sitting across from Kirsten eating a pie that made her stomach turn, so she pasted on a smile—more for Vitas's benefit than Kirsten's. She didn't know which depressed her more: that she was a forty-eight-year-old woman competing for the attentions of a man or that she was doing so against an Olympic-caliber flirt like Kirsten.

"Are sure is good?" Vitas said to Edina. "Look like is eating something poison." There it was: *sumzing*. It was charming—Vitas's brutal pronunciations, his tight-fisted grip on Slavic grammar—although Edina was disappointed in herself for thinking so. She took pride in her English, her fluent control of its ridiculous rules and inexplicable pronunciations, and before meeting Vitas had considered the headlong abuse of any language to be a failure of self-discipline or a sign of sloppiness.

"Everybody eat up," Kirsten said when each of them had a paper plate of mangled pie. Edina blew into her hands and rubbed them together, her pale fingers ashen, her nails purple.

Vitas drew out the flask and held it poised over the table. "Edina," he said, "this put feeling back in fingers, toes, ears, hair—everywhere." He poured a splash into her cider, then topped off his cup and Kirsten's.

Kirsten bolted her drink in a single swallow. Vitas roared with laughter and refilled her cup while Edina pushed the fragments of pie around her plate and sipped the cocktail of cider and vodka. In the far corner of the room she spotted some kind of outdated farm machinery—a scooped metal seat perched above crabbed fingers of bent steel. Edina could only guess how the contraption worked: Pulled behind a tractor? Dragged by a mule or ox? Her father and grandfather were doctors; she was at home with stainless steel and sterile surfaces but not with the rust-furred implements of farming. These were causes of injury and infection. These were the reasons why people came to see doctors.

Edina turned her head and sniffed at her shoulder. She could still smell the orchard, and she wanted to know if the scent hung in the air, or only in memory, or if it had penetrated the fabric of her coat.

"Does something smell funny?" Kirsten said.

"No, it's nothing," Edina said, quietly cursing Kirsten for noticing and cursing herself for giving Kirsten something to notice. Kirsten's eyes were trained on her, as harsh as bare bulbs. "It's just that smell in the orchard. It...lingers."

"You mean that sticky apple smell?" Kirsten's face lit up. "I totally know what you mean. It's so, I don't know—memorable. I took this psych class in college, and we talked about how smell is the sense that's most closely linked to memory, how certain smells can bring back these super-intense feelings in a way that hearing a voice or seeing a picture never can." She sipped her vodka, her eyes darting from Vitas to Edina over the rim of the cup. Kirsten had eyes like a china doll's: bright, almost luminous, and shot through with radiant splinters of brown glass. "This is going to sound crazy," she said, leaning into the table, "but I swear that smell always makes me think of the first time I had sex."

Edina almost dropped her cup. It was just as she had told Vitas: *She's always looking for an excuse to talk. And the girl will say anything!* While Edina stiffened in her seat, Vitas slapped the table and let loose another bark of laughter. At the next table, a man and a woman were parceling out doughnut halves to three red-cheeked boys. In the warmth of the café, snot ran freely from their noses. The children flinched, their hands frozen in mid-grasp at the sound of Vitas's laugh. Unaware and undeterred, Vitas clapped his hands like cymbals. "First love!" he said.

"I wouldn't call it love," Kirsten said. "I mean, at the time, sure—I was crazy about him. But I think I was just crazy, you know, the way you are when you're seventeen."

"Seventeen." Vitas rolled the word around in his mouth like hard candy, his eyes scanning the rafters high above. "Is crazy, crazy time."

Edina hoped that Kirsten's story would end there, with each of them silently contemplating the conjunction of *sex* and *seventeen*. Edina raised her cup to her lips. At seventeen, she had just started university. She was finally away from home and eager for the life she had always imagined was awaiting her in Sarajevo. But as the vodka slid down Edina's throat, Kirsten broke the silence.

"It was around this time of year," she said, "but up in Wisconsin. That's where I'm from. It's the state above Illinois. There's a lot of trees and hills up there; it's not flat like it is around here." She sipped once from her cup, then finished it off with a gulp.

"So anyway, there was this big Halloween party that my high school threw at one of the orchards outside Madison. There was music, hayrides, a big bonfire. Wait—" Kirsten swiveled her head from Vitas to Edina. "Do you guys know what Halloween is?"

They nodded.

"Just stop me if I say something that doesn't make sense," Kirsten said. Edina wanted to catch Vitas's eye, but she saw that he was already looking straight at her, one eyebrow raised, warning her: *Don't be so mean.* He twisted the top off the flask and poured a shot into Kirsten's cup. "I'm never sure how much you know about American culture," Kirsten said, "and I don't want to presume that of course you know what Halloween is or where Wisconsin is. Okay?" Kirsten's cheeks were flushed, her eyes glowing. She scanned their faces, ready for questions about local customs and Midwestern geography. Then she raised her cup, winked at Vitas, and downed the contents.

"So there was this big Halloween party, and there must have been two or three hundred kids there. I was a junior—that means third year of high school—and I was hanging out with this guy Todd, who was a senior and on the football team. He wasn't the quarterback or anything—"

She looked again from Edina to Vitas. "The quarterback is the big star on the football team. He's the one who throws the ball." She cocked her arm as if about to throw a perfect spiral. "Todd wasn't even that good, but he was cute and nice and whatever. It was high school." Vitas sipped from his cup and nodded, apparently satisfied with this explanation of her attraction to Todd.

"He had swiped a bottle of peppermint schnapps from his parents' liquor cabinet, and we were doing shots straight from the bottle. We'd hooked up a bunch of times, but we hadn't done it. I could tell he wanted to, but I think he was a virgin too so he wasn't too smooth."

"Poor Todd," Vitas said, shaking his head. "Is all the time wondering, *When, Kirsten? When?*"

"Hold your horses," she said, "I'm getting to that part. So anyway, the party was supposed to end at eleven, and by ten o'clock couples were disappearing into the orchard. Todd said we should go for a walk, look at the stars, that sort of thing, and I was like, *Sure*. The moon was out and it was a pretty warm night for October—we call it Indian summer, I don't know why. Anyway, it was hard to find a spot with a little privacy because every time you went to sit down under a tree there'd be two people totally going at it, and you'd be like, *Whoops, sorry*."

Kirsten was speaking more quickly, her words starting to slur. Edina had counted three shots from the vodka bottle since they sat down in the café, plus whatever Kirsten had had during the walk from the orchard—her lips where Edina's had been, tasting the sharp metal before the rush of vodka. As if reading Edina's mind, Kirsten nudged her cup closer to the flask, asking for a refill.

"So Todd and I are making out and blah-blah-blah and when he unbuttons my jeans I just think, *Why not?* I mean, there was more going through my head than that, but I liked him a lot and I *did* want to do it. I don't know. I'm sure the schnapps helped.

"So anyway, that smell. Todd's on top of me, and there's nowhere I can go that I don't have about a dozen apples poking me in the back. And that smell—rotten, but also kinda sweet—is everywhere. So I'm squirming around like crazy, which Todd probably thinks is because he's such a superstud, but really I was just trying to find a spot that was halfway comfortable." At the next table, the mother loudly gathered cups and shot acid-laced glances at Kirsten's back while the father pulled mittens over his sons' sugar-coated fingers.

"Lucky for me things didn't last very long. Like I said, Todd wasn't exactly Mr. Lover Man. Then on the way back to the fire, Todd let me wear his letter jacket, which I thought was sweet of him, but for the rest of the night I was pulling these mashed-up pieces of apple out of my hair, and it took like three showers to get rid of that smell. All in all, I guess it was pretty gross."

"Poor Todd," Vitas said. "So much to learn."

"Poor Todd!" Kirsten rapped Vitas on the arm, her face a full-lipped pout. "Todd turned out to be a jerk. Two weeks later he hooked up with a cheerleader."

Edina checked her watch. She was starting to think that it didn't matter when they returned to Evanston, because she had a pretty clear idea of Vitas's plans for the night. Maybe she had been missing the signs all along, and today was just another bead in a string of drinks and jokes and flirting and more.

Was this something Kirsten would have eventually told Edina all about on one of those mornings when she slouched in her doorway? Was this the story that a single question would have unlocked? Kirsten and Vitas: hooking up, making out, doing it, blah–blah–blah.

Edina gulped from her cup. What did she care if Kirsten and Vitas met every day for lovers' trysts? As long as they didn't interfere with her work, what did she care? Before today, she had barely thought of Vitas at all. He was that loud, crazy Lithuanian who was rarely in the office. He was always out "making interviews," as he called it, or stampeding the others to a bar. Soon she would be back in Sarajevo, back in her apartment, back at her job, doing all of the little things that kept life moving: making sure the magazine got to the printer on time; writing updates on the "Bosnian situation" for a variety of well-meaning and largely ignored NGOs; organizing panels to discuss displaced persons, civil society, right of return. A friend of hers had once said that Edina didn't have a career, she had an addiction—but it was an addiction that gave shape to her life.

"You're awfully quiet," Kirsten said, turning to Edina. With the way Kirsten could spin innocuous observations into questions, every word out of her mouth was a land mine. If Edina was quiet, then she must be thinking, and if something was worth thinking—Kirsten's philosophy seemed to be—then it was worth saying. Out loud. And preferably to a group of near-total strangers.

"So what's on your mind?" Kirsten said.

"Nothing really." She couldn't help looking for Vitas's hands.

One was on the table, cradling his cup, the other—the one closest to Kirsten—under the table. Unaccounted for.

"Nothing at all?" Kirsten said, slurring *nothing* into *nussing*.

"Nothing." Edina sharpened her pronunciation. She tried to make the word sound flatly Midwestern, but it came out loud and hard. Another word from her dictionary loomed: *brusque*.

"What about last night?" Kirsten said. She had invited Edina to join them for drinks after work, but Edina had said that she already had plans. "Did you do anything fun?"

"Nothing special." Edina's fingernails inscribed half-moons into the soft flesh of her palms.

"Did you go out?"

"Outside? No, it was too damp."

"But did you go out-out—you know, to a restaurant or a bar or a club?"

"Do you mean to discos?" She shook her head. "No, that's not for me."

"You know, that's really funny," Kirsten said. "Nobody says *disco* anymore."

"I was not trying to make a joke," Edina said.

"I just think it's a funny word: *disco*. You know, like in the seventies."

Edina looked up at Kirsten, expressionless. "It is just a word," she said. "I have never thought of it as funny before."

"Edina," Vitas chided her, "is not interrogation. Is two friends, talking."

"No, forget it," Kirsten said, raising her cup to her lips. "I told you she was like this." Edina was struck by how suddenly emotion rewrote the girl's features—one second, eyes lolling drunkenly in her head; the next, her cheeks were flushed and her eyes brimmed with hot tears.

"Like what?" Edina tried to sound innocent, even oblivious, but Kirsten's words burned with their suggestion of intimacy—of inside jokes and shared opinions. *I told you she was like this.*

"Like what?" Kirsten said, incredulous. "Like this!" She spit out the words. Her fingers were splayed, as if she were dumping two months of snubs, audible sighs, and indiscreetly rolled eyes back into Edina's lap. "You never want to tell me anything about who you are, or what you do, or what you like."

Edina swallowed hard, clearing the burr from her throat. "There isn't much to tell."

"There must be something." *Sump-thin;* now the girl was really butchering her own language.

"There's nothing," Edina said defensively, almost apologetically. "Just life."

"Just life is plenty!" Kirsten said. "But you won't tell me anything. You won't even be nice to me."

This was all a joke, wasn't it? *You silly girl,* she wanted to say. She had seen this look before, on the face of her four-year-old niece, sulking because Auntie Edina wouldn't read her *one more bedtime story!* But as her eyes darted from Vitas back to Kirsten, she saw that he agreed with the girl. Hadn't he been saying the same thing in the orchard? And now Edina had to say something, *sumzing, sump-thin* to end the brutal silence—to show that *she* wasn't the monster. She wished that she did have a secret double life; at least she'd have something to say. The truth was far more mundane.

Since coming to Chicago, she'd spent a lot of time in her apartment.

She walked by the lake, which some days was soft and gray as old flannel and others as green and whitecapped as a shattered windshield.

She wrote her father long letters. She was his only daughter, and he complained that the apartment they shared in Sarajevo was too quiet and there were few distractions to help him pass the time—just the cat, his medical journals, and the bootleg CDs of Bartók and Prokofiev that Edina had bought from the street vendors.

On weekends she rode the El south to Belmont and then bounced back north on the Brown Line to Lincoln Square, where stout matrons lined up at the butcher for *cevapcici* and where a man from Banja Luka made pizzas topped with spicy wedges of *sudak*.

But this wasn't what Kirsten had waited so long to hear: that Edina was homesick and spent far too much time moping—time she knew she'd regret when she was back home, besieged by office deadlines and her father's questions about where she was, when she was coming home, and what she was making for dinner.

"Kirsten, I do like you," Edina said, dragging the words out of her throat. For a split second she thought about patting Kirsten's hand, even giving it a firm squeeze.

"No," Kirsten said, her eyes hard and bright as mica. "You

don't. And you've had this black cloud hanging over you all day. If spending time with the rest of us makes you so miserable, then why did you even come?"

Kirsten was pressing her advantage, and Edina felt her patience drying up. "If I had known about the change of plans, perhaps I would have stayed at home."

"So now you hate apple-picking too?" Vitas put a hand on Kirsten's shoulder, the hand that had been beneath the table, and murmured into her ear. She swatted at him. "I don't want to calm down! I want to know what her problem is."

"My problem?" Edina said. Blood burned in her face, scouring out the last traces of embarrassment and leaving behind a core of vivid anger. "You want to know what my problem is? You want to know what's on my mind? I'll tell you. That rotten-apple smell—the one that reminds you of Halloween parties and sex with the quarterback—"

"Todd wasn't the quarter—"

Edina cut her short with a look she hoped was *withering*. She sat back abruptly, her fingers tented over her nose. She took a deep breath and told herself to be calm, to take it slowly, not to let it get away from her.

"We had a war," she said finally, looking directly at Kirsten, "before you were born. When the fighting started, everyone I knew said we would be safe. There was a garrison of the Yugoslav army in our town, and the new Bosnian president said that they would protect us from the militias. He believed that the soldiers would follow his orders. Of course that's not what happened.

"We had heard the rumors about the camps, but it didn't seem possible. This was Europe; things like that didn't happen anymore. Then one day we heard on the radio that the Serbs were coming. We had a day, maybe two to prepare. Most of the people were packing, preparing to go to Tuzla or one of the other safe areas, but a group of us refused to go. We just couldn't believe this was happening. This was our home. We were building a new country." Edina lifted her cup. The vodka was like a spark in her throat.

"The Serbs came in the morning, ready to liberate the town from the Turks. That's what they called us—what they called anyone who wasn't one of them. When we saw that they were riding in Yugoslav army trucks, we realized that no one was going to protect us. There were so many of them, and what did we have? A few old guns, some hunting rifles—and we weren't soldiers. All we were was young." Kirsten was leaning forward, her eyes wide. "I was your age, Kirsten. I had just graduated from university. I wanted to be a poet." Edina's cup was empty, and she waited as Vitas refilled it. After he screwed the top back on the flask, he folded his hands heavily on the table.

"We drove as fast as we could out of town, and when we saw roadblocks ahead, we abandoned the cars and fled into the hills. We thought the Serbs would ignore us—they wanted us to leave; we left." Edina stared across the room at the stiff, spooked faces of the pioneers. "After an hour, we came upon an orchard. There were about thirty of us, men and women both. We were halfway through the orchard when sniper fire started. The trees were like the ones here—short, the branches low to the ground—and we hid wherever we could. I was with my fiancé, but when the shooting started we were separated. He had given me an old shotgun, but that was foolishness. I had never fired a gun in my life, and the trees were so dense that it was impossible to see what was happening even five or ten meters away—just bullets coming through the branches. Then mortars started exploding all around, and when that stopped, the Chetniks moved in on foot. We could hear the sound of their rifles—automatics, Kalashnikovs—going *pop-pop-pop*. The only thing to do was stay low and shoot at anyone with good boots—the kind the army had given to the militias.

"Because of the war, none of the fruit had been picked, and the ground was covered with rotten apples. For hours I crawled through that mush. Hiding, waiting, then crawling some more. By the time the sun was down, the Serbs moved on and I reached the forest at the edge of the orchard. I waited all night for my fiancé or one of the others, and then at dawn I started walking alone. At noon I found a refugee convoy moving toward Sarajevo, but the trucks kept breaking down, and there were checkpoints, and it took eighteen hours to get to the city. All that time, the smell was in my skin, my hair, my mouth, everywhere. No matter how much I scrubbed, the smell wouldn't go away." Edina bolted down what vodka remained in her cup. "So today, when you were picking apples and thinking about Wisconsin and Halloween and Todd the quarterback, that's what was on my mind."

Tears traced snail tracks down Kirsten's face. "I am so, so sorry," she said. "If I had known—"

"You couldn't have," Edina said. It was some comfort to know that whatever Kirsten said next, it would not begin with *Do you know what that reminds me of?* Vitas handed Kirsten a wadded paper napkin, which she used to dab at her eyes. His jaw was set, his eyes narrow. He looked like one of those quiet, solid Scandinavians who lived across the Baltic, men carved from ice.

"Is good time to go home," Vitas said.

VITAS DROVE, EDINA rode in front, and Kirsten passed out in the backseat. Vitas assured Edina that he knew the way; all they had to do was go east until they hit the lake, and from there it would be a simple right or left turn to bring them to Evanston. Edina found a classical music station on the radio and turned it up loud enough to dispel any obligation to make conversation. Vitas kept his eyes on the road, his face illuminated by the headlights of on-coming traffic.

Twenty minutes into the drive, his eyes lingered in the rearview mirror, taking in the scene in the backseat. He watched the road for a while, then lowered the volume on the radio.

"Is okay if talking?" His voice startled Edina. She had been wondering if she had said too much—wondering if two months in the States was affecting her in ways she hadn't expected. "All-American apple pie makes very tired, and talking is good for staying awake."

A smile pricked the corners of her mouth. "So it's the pie, not the vodka?"

"Of course," Vitas said. "Vodka give energy. But pie? Look what it do to Kirsten."

The road was four lanes in each direction, bordered by parking lots and department stores. The line of streetlights strobed off the hood of the car. "You're not going to tell me about your first time, are you?" she said.

Vitas chuckled before he spoke. "Well, is not like Kirsten first time," he said. "Is first time in love. I think is different." He sounded almost shy, skirting around the edges of the story rather than plunging headlong into the telling. There was a sudden burst of sound as Vitas rolled his window down an inch, followed by the flare of his lighter. He had both hands off the wheel, steadying it with his knees. He stoked a cigarette to life extravagantly, as if it were a cigar.

"There was girl, long times ago, when I am at university," he said. He ashed his cigarette against the top of the window; the sparks raced away from the car. "How to say how beautiful? Hair is like mink—so dark, but in the light, is glowing. Dark eyes too. Dark as coffee after long night of vodka."

"You're the one who should have been a poet," she said.

He made a noncommittal noise—a clipped hum—and jetted a plume of smoke toward the window. "During this times, is many things for poets to write. We believe are making new world. We are seeing Berlin Wall, Solidarity, Havel. Now is our turn, yes? I making speeches, writing articles, leading marches, always saying same thing: 'Lithuania must be free!'" Vitas chopped the air in front of him, and the tip of his cigarette arced like neon. "Sometimes crowds so big that I use bull's horn, and everyone is cheering. I wave arms and cheering is getting louder. When troops come for first time, we saying, 'Go home! Go back to Moscow!' They have guns and we have banners, but we do not care. We are young, and is crazy time."

"The young rebel," Edina said, smiling in the darkness. She pictured Vitas, his hair thicker, his features more angular, his skin flushed in the long days of a Baltic summer. "The girls must have loved you."

"Girls. Well. Now are bringing me back to start of story." He checked the rearview mirror—not a darting glance, but slowly, casually. "All the time I making speeches and saying Lithuania must be free I am in love with this girl—"

"The girl with the mink hair?"

"Of course," he said. "Is most beautiful girl at university. Also sweetest. Also smartest. And here is funny thing: she love me too."

"I thought you said she was smart." Edina played along—she felt the rhythm of their walk in the orchard returning—but her heart wasn't in it. And despite herself, she counted every time he looked in the rearview mirror and wondered if Kirsten's hair could be described as mink.

"Smart about everything, but not love," he said. "But I do not complain. Is angel. Is bringing me coffee in the morning and vodka at night and rubbing my feet after marches and listening to speeches and telling me how to say better this or that. Her name was Nadia Volkonsky. You are listening? Volkonsky. Very Russian name. Very un-Lithuanian name. It never matters. Nadia is born in Vilnius, and her heart is one hundred percents Lithuanian.

"But then is January, and many more troops coming, and soldiers are killing demonstrators. All of us going crazy. We are pulling down statues of Russian heroes and tearing down street signs in Russian. Anything looking Russian or sounding Russian or smelling Russian: all must go. And I hear voices behind my back say, 'How can Vitas be for real when is banging that Russian slut?' I saying to them all to fuck off, but their words stay in my head. My country belongs to Russia for too long, and now it must be ours, must be free, must be . . ." He paused for a moment, the streetlights illuminating his face in slow pulses. "Must be clean."

Edina shifted in her seat. The faint sound of a piano seeped from the speakers.

"So there is me, big man in movement, and I see Nadia, and I should see angel, because angel is what she is, but what I seeing now is Russian devil. I say to her things are no good. She is not making me happy. Is not understanding me. All bullshit things. Then one day at protest leaders' meeting, I start big argument with her, and in front of everyone I saying to her, 'Go home to Moscow!' Is same thing we saying to soldiers. She looks for someone to tell me I am asshole—is roomful of her friends, her comrades—but nobody says nothing."

Nobody says nuzzing. Edina mouthed the words to herself.

"Is standing there, my angel, with tears in her eyes. I feel those eyes, hot like coal, but I am not looking at her. I am looking down. Waiting for her to leave. We all do same. All of us heroes of revolution. So brave in streets, but in our hearts, cowards."

Edina listened to the metronomic tick of the road against the tires. They were moving east along a road populated with gas stations and low, flat office parks. Wisps of exhaust reached upward into the cold night air. After a red light, the gas stations gave way to a dense stand of trees, a black mass of wadded shadows that lined the road.

"You want last chapter?" Vitas said, his voice breaking the silence, again surprising Edina. "For long time, I am thinking I ruin her life. Nadia is sweet, so kind, and see: This is what happens. It kills her, I am thinking, for me to throw her away. But ten years ago I am in Saint Petersburg, making interviews. I going to café and am seeing woman with husband and little girl. Woman is beautiful, and from clothes and hair I can tell is rich too. And husband doesn't look like old, fat Russian. Rich, but not mafia." Vitas lit another cigarette, quickly this time, and took a long drag. "Of course is Nadia, and is singing song with little girl and when is done husband claps and gives little girl big hug. Is perfect, yes? Is maybe life I could had. So what I do? I get up. I run. Run like chair is on fire. And when I get to street I still running, and everyone thinking I am crazy drunk. Or thief." He paused, and the tip of his cigarette glowed. "Or maybe," he said, "man who is seeing ghost."

They were on a street without stoplights, angling south alongside the railroad, the lake roiling darkly behind tall maples and quiet mansions.

"Now you see," Vitas said, and then added: "Is something you should know."

THEY CARRIED KIRSTEN into her apartment and put her in bed with a glass of water on the nightstand and a shopping bag near her head. Edina did not ask Vitas how he knew where Kirsten lived.

When they left, Edina shoved her hands deep in her pockets for the walk to their building. One fist gripped the whistle on her key ring—part of her welcome package from Kirsten, who told her that blowing the whistle would scare away muggers or rapists and summon the police to her side. It was that simple.

They covered the distance without speaking, their breath rising in spectral puffs on the darkened side streets. Yellow light warmed the windows of the houses. Televisions spilled blue pulses onto the empty porches. The trees were almost bare. Wet leaves were pasted to the sidewalk, while the dry ones could be heard scrabbling across the road in the sharp, lakeward wind. In silence they climbed the three flights of stairs to where their apartment doors faced each other across a narrow, dimly lit hallway.

"Edina, you know what I trying to say in car?"

She had her key in her hand. She was tired, her limbs heavy and useless, like a parachutist fallen into the ocean, struggling for air as her chute fills with water. "I'm sorry," she said. "It's been a very long day. I don't think I'm any good at talking right now." She wanted to tell him that it was unnecessary—this confession, this explanation. Wasn't it enough that Kirsten was young and pretty? Did he also have to see in her the face of a love he had abandoned? Edina didn't blame him for trying to relive happier moments, before regret had taken a bite out of his heart. She just didn't want to hear his attempts to justify it.

"I am not clear," he said, screwing up his face. "If can speak like you, would be simple to say."

She saw in his eyes that he wanted her to make this easier for him, but nothing was ever easy.

"I hoping," he said, "that you are not thinking I am like those men. The men with good boots."

Those men? She groped for something to say. "You—you didn't kill anyone."

"Yes, is different," he said, shifting from one foot to the other. "But is also same."

She looked down the corridor, the line of doors receding in the distance. Her key was in her hand. All she wanted was to be inside, to close the door on this day.

Vitas leaned closer. "Is what I trying to say in car," he said. "I want to be honest. And is why I tell you about Nadia—because you are alike her. Brave."

"Me?" she said. "But I thought—what about Kirsten?"

"The girl?" He shook his head. "I not understand."

She was beginning to feel dizzy—all that vodka and nothing to eat all day—and with one hand blindly sought the knob of her door. "I'm sorry," she said again, turning her back on him. "I'm very tired. I must—I need—good night." She unlocked the door, the whistle jangling against her keys. She knew Vitas was standing behind her, but without looking back she slipped inside her apartment.

The glass dome of the peephole flickered when Vitas's apartment spilled light into the hallway, then blinked when his door closed. The only sound was the rattle of steam rising in the radiators. Although it was dark in her apartment, she squeezed her eyes shut, as if that could stop the tears from coming. Sobs constricted her throat and she slid to the floor, where she hugged her knees tight to her chest.

She wasn't brave. That part had come out all wrong, and now it was worse than a lie. She wasn't brave, and she had tried to hold something back for herself, but all she had done was make a mess of everything. She wasn't brave, and her fiancé—sweet, serious Satko—didn't just disappear. They were separated when the first bullets struck, but all through the sniper fire and the mortar rounds, they had called to each other. She would shout his name and wait for his reply, then crawl through the stony crab apples and fetid mush toward the sound of him answering, "Didi! Didi!" Neither of them dared to stand because of the snipers, and for an hour she heard the distant, throaty huff of the mortars followed by the spray of shrapnel and splintered wood over her head. They called each other's names, but the terrain was steep and deeply rutted and they never seemed to draw any closer.

Satko called her name even after Edina saw the boots crushing the fallen fruit. She wanted to yell to him one last time to be quiet, to tell him the soldiers were coming, but when she saw those boots in the next row of trees she knew that any sound would give her away. She gripped the stock of the shotgun. She could kill the man closest to her, but there would be more, and the blast would lead them right to her. Amid the web of branches under one of the trees she curled herself into a ball and inwardly begged Satko to do the same. To hide. To wait. To bury her name deep in his throat and let it lie there, silent, where it could not betray him.

This Is Not a Love Song

She was Kitty to her parents, Katherine to the nuns in high school, Kate when she was in college. But to anyone who knew her then—Chicago in the first years of the nineties, her hands tearing at her guitar like a kid unwrapping a Christmas present—she had already become Kat.

Like the rest of the horde of art students and rockers-in-training, we lived in Wicker Park, where rents were low and apartments doubled as studios, rehearsal spaces, black-box theaters, and flophouses. The park itself was still a rusty triangle of scalded grass littered with needles and broken bottles. It would be a few years before the new trees and the swing sets and the DIE YUPPIE SCUM stencils on the smooth-bricked three-flats; before the press would hype Chicago as "the next Seattle," and record-company types started skulking around the bars. Back then, there weren't any boutiques on Damen selling five-hundred-dollar sweaters—just bodegas, auto-body shops, and empty storefronts whose faded signs whispered of plumbing supplies and cold storage.

Later there would be the brief flurry of albums and magazine covers, but back then the only people paying attention to her were the music nerds on the lookout for the next band you hadn't heard of and the rock critic from the free weekly who wrote mash-note reviews of any girl with a guitar. And me, of course, but by then I'd been paying attention to her for so long that I'd started to make a career out of it.

Interior. Stairwell. Evergreen Avenue loft.

She stands in the doorway, a ghost outlined by the yawning black of the stairwell. She looks drained, which is how she often looked in those days. Her arms are folded across her chest, and her skin bleeds into the T-shirt, white on white. Her hair must have been black then, because in the picture it's fused with the empty space around her, and her face really pops: jaw set, teeth bared, eyes canted to the side, as if the shutter caught her the second before she spit out some curse. Maybe this was the night the van got torched by our next-door neighbors—teenage Latin Kings or Latin Lovers or Latin Disciples, we hadn't yet figured out how to read their tags. Maybe it was the night the bass player told Kat he was going to law school. Or maybe she'd just been ambushed by Casimir the landlord wanting to know, *For sure, no joking, when you pay me my rent, huh? When you pay me my rent?* You can say that the way her body burns a hole in the middle of the image is just a photographer's trick, a little darkroom magic to saturate the blacks and flush everything to the whitest white, and you'd be right. But you can't deny that she's pissed.

Interior. Basement of Kat's parents' house. River Forest, Illinois.

If you can't imagine Kat in the gray skirt and Peter Pan collar required by the nuns at our all-girls high school, it's probably because you've never seen the pictures I took when I was the president and only dues-paying member of the photography club and Kat was spending afternoons and weekends punching out songs in her parents' basement and running them through the four-track she bought with a summer's worth of babysitting money. She was my only subject—my muse, you could say—but that was because she was the only one who would sit still while I fussed over lenses and light readings and angles. It wasn't patience—even then she was focused; even then she was very good at tuning out background noise. I took rolls and rolls of film of her bent over her guitar, her hair a veil over her eyes, her lips soundlessly counting out the beat. Then I'd disappear for days of red-light seclusion in my studio, which my parents insisted on calling the laundry room. A set of these pictures, soulful black-and-whites mostly, spiked with a few hallucinatory color shots, won the school art prize our senior year and had the added bonus of convincing every girl in our graduating class that we were a couple. It's too bad we weren't; maybe we wouldn't have been so lonely, so frustrated, so perpetually amped up.

Interior. Fireside Bowl. Fullerton Avenue.

Kat is onstage, surrounded by cigarette smoke and crowd steam, her eyes raked up at the low black ceiling. The smoke drifts into the shafts of light pouring from the Tinkertoy overhead rig, gives a shape to the air, makes visible the currents. You can see the way the heat from the crowd rises and then bends back on itself in ripples and swirls. For all the movement on the floor, from shoe-gazer swaying to manic pogoing to grand-mal moshing, the real action is above, where the air surges with color—candy-apple red and freeze-pop green, children-at-play yellow and police-light blue. Not that she ever looked at the crowd when she sang. The eyes of other people distracted her; the way those eyes begged for instant intimacy wasn't just an imposition, it was an affront. An assault, even.

She didn't look into the crowd, she looked over it, at some safe, empty spot on a far wall or a point on the ceiling where hands and faces could not reach. When she first started playing out in clubs where there was no stage, just a space on the floor to set up, her insistence on staring at the ceiling or squeezing her eyes shut tight gave her the look of some mad, ecstatic saint. People said she was blind, or epileptic, or terminally shy. Whatever they believed, they were talking about her, and she needed that kind of an advantage—that lingering hold on the crowd's mayfly attention—if she didn't want to get lumped in with every other band thrashing through its twenty-five minutes. (*Which band? The one with the freaky girl singer with the messed-up eyes? Oh yeah, they were pretty good.*)

Once she moved up to places with a stage that set her above the crowd, her eyes didn't have to roll so far back in her head to find that tranquil spot in the ceiling. Some people even kidded themselves into thinking that she was looking at them in those rare moments when her eyes flicked down to check her crabbed, chord-making fingers on the neck of her guitar. But she wasn't willing to share what she was feeling with anyone, not if sharing meant locking eyes with some other face out there in the dark and exchanging a smile or some acknowledgment that, hey, we're both in this moment together. Because that would have wrecked it. For her, I mean.

Box 5, spool 3.

MALE VOICE: What's her deal, anyway?

KAT: [*inaudible*]

M.V.: Because it's weird.

KAT: [*inaudible*]

M.V.: How am I supposed to do that? I can't turn around without her going *click-click-click*. It's like she's a spy or something.

KAT: She's not spying on you. She doesn't give a shit about you.

M.V.: Then why is she always taking my fucking picture?

KAT: Because she's spying on *me*. You're just . . . scenery.

School portrait. Seventh grade. Ascension Catholic School. Oak Park, Illinois. Kat smiles, lips together, to hide her braces. Photographer unknown.

If you wanted to go back to the very beginning, you would have to start with the days when her brother Gerry wanted to be Jimmy Page and Robert Plant all in one and his best friend had a drum kit so there was no question who got to be John Bonham. Gerry liked Led Zeppelin because they were loud and their album covers had secret symbols and some of the lyrics made references to *The Lord of the Rings*. He explained what the symbols meant, but he said she wouldn't really get it until she had read all of Tolkien, including *The Silmarillion*. Kat hadn't been able to get through *The Hobbit*. That's a kid's book, he told her. It doesn't mention the Valar or Númenor or any of the important stuff.

He told Kat she could play bass or get lost. Kat knew that she was only in the band until her brother made another friend, but even at thirteen she sensed that Gerry was socially radioactive and that this provided her with some security, band-wise.

Fast-forward ten years and Gerry, grown up and living on the Gold Coast, used to stop by all the time. He was in sales, though most of his job seemed to consist of taking out-of-towners to dinner at one of the steak houses that served plate-size slabs of beef and where they practically let you select the cow to be slaughtered for your dining pleasure. Once his clients were glutted with porterhouse and cabernet, they would barhop the strip clubs, but if the night ever broke up early—say, before two a.m.—Gerry would show up at our place, half drunk and ready to be entertained.

Typical night: We would come home to find him planted on the couch finishing off our last bottle of beer. He had swiped a key, and getting the locks changed was an enormous hassle.

"Hey," he'd say. "You're all out of beer."

Or this: "One of your neighbors gave me the stink-eye. What have they got against white people?"

Or this: "You've got to let me jam with you sometime. Come

on, I'm just messing with you. I know you wouldn't want me upstaging you. See, I'm still messing with you."

Another time, his clients canceled dinner. He'd taken them to a day game at Wrigley and they'd had too much Old Style, too much sun. Kat was going out to see a new band at Medusa's and Gerry volunteered to come with.

"But you have to stop doing that 'Gerry with a G' thing," Kat told him. "Every time you meet somebody, it's 'Hi, Gerry with a G, Gerry with a G.'"

"Force of habit." He was examining the innards of the refrigerator, the augury of the bored and distracted.

"So kick the habit," she said. "You're not selling anything here."

He looked at her like he was disappointed, like she was too stupid to get it. "Kitty, I'm selling Gerry with a G."

He spent the rest of the night with a big grin on his face, telling stories about Kat when she was in grade school and clearing up misconceptions about the band he had once led—how they specialized not only in Led Zeppelin, but in Rush, Black Sabbath, and Deep Purple. Whenever there was a change of venue, Gerry with a G would launch into the same material with a new crowd of banddudes, hangers-on, and the eyelinered riffraff who we called friends.

Interior. The Empty Bottle. Western Avenue.
She hit the stage in an English Beat T-shirt and black jeans cropped just below the knee. Capris, you could have called them, if that didn't seem such a kicky, genteel name for pants that had SAVE ME painted in white on one thigh and FUCK YOU on the other. The

crowd loved it, but by then she really didn't need to try so hard to get their attention. After every show, guys came up to her, their fanboy hearts aflutter, and told her about a new band that she should check out or asked what she thought about this or that album. They always talked too loud and their eyes were bright and unblinking, like cultists inviting her to spend the weekend at their compound. It was just music geeks showing off, she knew that, but she also knew that as they talked about mail-order-import B-sides, they hoped that she would be so impressed that she'd drag one of them back to her place for a wild night of indie-rock sex. There were a lot of reasons why that would never happen, and high on that list was Kat's conviction that these were guys who knew exactly what song they'd want on the stereo through the whole sordid episode. Most of them probably carried a mixtape—"Jason's Sex Mix '92"—for just that purpose.

Later, after her first album dropped, *Spin* ran a short, front-of-the-book Q&A with her. When they asked about some of the dirtier, angstier breakup songs, Kat played coy and said that she was, at twenty-five, still a virgin. A complete lie, but you should have seen the music nerds. I told her that she had to stop messing with the heads of her core demographic, but during the first show after the article ran, she added a revved-up cover of "Like a Virgin" to the set list. Chaos ensued.

Exterior. Night. Café Voltaire. Clark Street. Hand-painted sign reads ART TONIGHT.
There was a guy named Giles, who we used to call J. Geils whenever we thought he couldn't hear us. He wasn't an artist

and he wasn't in a band but he was always around and he had the kind of dark energy that singers and guitarists try hard to project, and this made him both attractive and repellent, depending on your own particular polarity. I, for one, was negatively inclined, but Kat got very, very into him—so into him that she stopped calling him J. Geils and started to give me a *Really? You're still doing that?* look whenever I used his nickname, this thing we had made together.

Giles and his friends had money, but they didn't have jobs. They exchanged elaborate handshakes, and they had already been places—Thailand, Prague, Chile, Morocco—that marked them as secret agents or trust-fund kids or time-traveling citizens of some future world. None of this seemed to bother Kat. Soon I began to notice that when Kat said "we," more often than not she was referring to her and Giles, not her and me.

I was forced to cultivate other interests. I got an idea about making sound collages and let a reel-to-reel run in the loft, picking up doors slamming and the toilet flushing and stray bits of conversation. I thought about studying for some kind of professional-school exam. I started writing a play based entirely on personal ads in the *Reader* but never got much farther than the title: *Men Seeking Women.*

One night I attended an opening for the work of former rivals from the Art Institute in a basement coffee shop where canvases covered in chewed paper and dental floss were mercilessly lit by thrift-store lamps. I smiled and cheek-kissed and appeared to ponder, but it was the lamps that demanded my attention: a chipped urn of pale blue that cast jug-eared shadows, a nightmare-faced ceramic monkey in a gold-buttoned waistcoat, a rooster whose comb rose like a blood-soaked hat. I had something like a revelation: Why did we keep making new art, and so much of it so bad, when we were surrounded by work that needed only the proper context to shine? So that was me—epiphanic from looking at bad arts and better crafts.

I came home and found the television on, the loft awash in noise and blue light. Kat, Giles-less, pulled the sleeve of her T-shirt tight to dab at her eyes.

I asked her if she was crying.

Kat sniffled. "It's the TV. Something on the stupid TV made me cry, okay?"

I looked at the screen: *Cheers*. "What, did Norm die?"

"Just forget it, all right?" She took a deep breath and loudly exhaled. "Giles and I had a—a fight." She rolled her eyes. Stupid. Like something from high school, if she had dated anyone in high school.

"A big one?"

"Pretty big." She turned her face to me, straight on, and I saw the red welt blazing beneath her eye. My hand went to the body of my camera, as if by instinct, before I pulled it back.

"Can we start calling him J. Geils again?"

I thought she was going to tell me to get lost or go fuck myself. It was fifty-fifty on that one; that's how into him she had been. Instead I got that lopsided smile of hers, the one I could never catch on film, the one I'd pay a million dollars to see again.

Still life. Evergreen Avenue loft.

Call this one *A Study in Misguided Affection:* A table with a Formica top. An ashtray logjammed with cigarettes. Three mismatched. glasses containing various liquids—clear, pale yellow, dark brown— in varying amounts. A pile of scattered coins: nine quarters, two nickels, one dime. A CTA fare card. A spray of keys. A stack of bills—utility, credit card, student loan—unpaid, unopened. A large manila envelope, jagged-mouthed along one edge, addressed in cursive to Miss Katherine Conboy. A folded page from the *Tribune* classifieds; circled in red is an ad for a music teacher/band director at Northfield High School and next to the ad, also in red, Kat's mother has written, *Think about it!!!! XOXO Mom.*

Color mock-up. Cover of the band's debut album, *Chica-Go-Go*. Kat and the others slouch against a wall, à la the Ramones.

I dated this guy Milo for longer than I should have. He was thin without being too bony. His hair was neither too shaggy nor too expensively cut. His whole wardrobe was short-sleeve button-downs—thrift-store issue, though he had a good eye for it. The patterns were neither too dorky nor too Euro. He wasn't too bright, but he wasn't an idiot either. That was Milo. He was neither too this nor too that. He was, for a time, just right. We called him Baby Bear.

He did something with computers during the day and at night he played trumpet in a ska-Krautrock outfit called Rudie Kant Fail that had yet to land any of the big bookings that he believed were their due. He bemoaned "the tyranny of verse-chorus-verse" to anyone who would listen, even though it was a swipe at the music Kat was playing. Milo was the first person I knew who had an e-mail address, but since no one else had one, it was pretty useless. He probably works in an office now and every time some entry-level programmer gets the grand tour of the cubicles, someone will elbow the new guy and say, *You ever heard of Kat Conboy? That singer who died? Milo over there used to date her roommate.* And the new guy will be like, *No way,* because he'll look at Milo and he'll picture Kat and he'll go, *Does. Not. Compute.* But back then, when we were young, before 99 percent of the people we knew moved on to Life Plan B, it did make some kind of sense.

Milo was in the loft on the night Kat told me that she'd met the guy from Matador, the one who would eventually sign the band and release their first album. The Matador guy had gotten hold of one of her cassettes—she had given them to two people, in other bands, and within a month they'd multiplied like rabbits. She was viral before there was viral. She had run up the stairs and her eyes were glowing when she told me, but the light went out when she saw Milo was in the loft. He'd heard everything. "Dat's da bomb!" he said.

Kat told him to pipe down. That's just what she said—*Pipe down*—which was something her father used to say. Milo was loud, it was late, and Kat had grown tired of his penchant for saying things like "da bomb" and "word" and "fly" and "fresh." She thought it made him sound foolish, like the joke was on him. She told him it was a question of authenticity.

"But you're talking M to the A to the T to the Dor. That's dope."

Matador *was* dope. If they were interested in Kat, it was a sign of good things to come.

Kat shrugged, and I could tell that she wished she hadn't said anything. Not in front of him. She looked at me like I'd tricked her, letting her share this good news when Milo was right around the corner, waiting to ruin it.

Exterior. Daylight. Rock Island Centennial Bridge. Kat leans over the guardrail, spitting into the Mississippi.

This is how she explained it to me: There just aren't enough hours in the day. But then you figure out that if you take the right pills, there still aren't enough hours but there are more, and you need all the time you can get. You don't take the pills to feel good; you take them because if you don't you'll be miserable about all of the things you don't have the time or the energy or, let's face it, the *strength* to do. Because working a job to pay for bad food and a lousy apartment and banged-up equipment and posters for every show takes time, and rehearsing takes time, and touring takes time. Oh, does touring take time. Do you know how long the drive to the Quad Cities is? Hours in the van to be the third act at an all-ages show in a broken-down roller rink, followed by an immediate and equally long return trip because half the band will get shit-canned from their name-tag jobs if they miss one more shift. And if this is an honest-to-God tour, a go-out-on-the-road-and-don't-come-back-for-a-week-or-two tour, then you will be sapped in other ways: Sleeping on one couch after another, or on a series of floors, getting acquainted with the many verminous regional varieties of upholstery and shag carpet. Figuring out if there's anyone at the show worth fucking in exchange for a night in an actual bed. Remembering where the van is parked so you don't get marooned in Carbondale, or Macomb, or Terre Haute.

And to bring this back around to the pills and their utility: How else does anyone stay awake at the wheel for a drive like that, a superhuman effort necessary to keep the members of Pope Joan from going the way of Buddy Holly, Ritchie Valens, and the Big Bopper, albeit in a flightless, much-less-famous, not–inspiring–the–next–"Miss American Pie" sort of way?

So, yes, pharmaceutical intervention is necessary for the drive across the murderous Midwestern prairie, and when you start to think about it, you realize that every day asks for a kind of hero-ism—and even, at times, for the kind of effort that would grind lesser mortals to chalk. How else do you start a day on three hours of sleep and then endure a double shift at your copy-shop job and then a few hours at a sparsely peopled backroom club showing support for a friend's latest band (and inking with your presence an unspoken contract that he will do the same for you)—and only then, after seventeen or eighteen misspent waking hours, will you finally be able to get to the part of the day that matters? Because if you don't do it—if you don't sit your ass on the busted springs of the couch with your guitar cradled in your lap and a spiral note-book in front of you bristling with gibberish that you need to wrestle into lyrics; if you don't fit words to the tune that has been ticking in your head all day long before it evaporates, leaving only a crust of failure around the bathtub rim that is your skull; if you don't do *this,* then you will go to bed—a collapse, a surrender, call it what you will—filled with the knowledge, now more apparent than ever, that you are a fraud, a faker, a failure. So if a handful of red or yellow or green or blue pills, administered daily, can keep that gnawing thought at bay *and* make it possible to get those sounds out of your head and into the world, you really have to ask: What's the harm in that?

Box 7, spool 2.

KAT: Hello? Hel—Dad, is that? Dad? Dad, it's Kat—I mean, it's Kitty. Kitty. Kit-ty. Your daughter, Kitty. Yes, like kitty cat. No, a person. I'm a person. Remember, from Christmas? I gave you . . . uh-huh. Uh-huh. Uh. Huh. Dad, is Mom there? Is she there with you? Mom. You know, the woman. The woman who lives in the house. Yes, the lady with short hair. From dinnertime, yes. No, it's not dinnertime. Not yet. No, it's not. Not yet. Is the woman—is—hello? Hello? Mom? What the hell, Mom? When did Dad start answering the phone? I didn't—I—I'm not *accusing* you of anything—

Exterior. Night. Rainbo Club. Damen Avenue.

One night Kat told me we needed to go out. The band had been touring the Midwest—Iowa City, Cedar Rapids, Champaign-Urbana, both Bloomingtons—and we hadn't seen much of each other. She told me she missed me. She told me she had been a bad friend. She told me the only way to drive out a nail is with another nail—that was another of her father's sayings. Her stated goal was to find me a better, post-Milo boyfriend, or at least a reasonably unembarrassing one-nighter, but sometime after all the two a.m. bars closed and the dirty stay-outs migrated to the last of the four a.m. bars, we ran into Giles. In the best of the pictures from that night, Kat had just made contact with his jaw, and his head was twisted to one side like someone was trying to screw it off his neck. It had rained earlier in the evening, and behind us the neon lay on the puddles like splattered milk. To the left of Giles was his new girlfriend, the lead singer in a band called Violet Beau; she was wearing a silver-lamé jacket that shone like woven crystal. Her face appears on film as a collage of spheres and circles: Her eyes so wide that they seem lidless, her mouth rounded into a big O. If I remember it right, she was about to say *Oh, snap!,* which probably made Kat want to punch her too. Authenticity, after all.

Exterior. Night. Lincoln Avenue just west of Halsted. A line of people; a man checking IDs with a small flashlight.
Ask anyone who knew Lounge Ax and they'll tell you: The place was a shoe box. If you believed the fire marshal's sign posted near the door, it couldn't hold more than a hundred and fifty people, but most nights the bodies were wedged chest to back and there could have been three or four hundred from the window facing the street to the front of the stage. Risers lined the walls, prime spots where you could see above the bobbing heads to the back of the postage-stamp stage and where you were less likely to get groped.

I have a picture from that night, before the really bad stuff, or the really good stuff, depending on your point of view. She has just finished her set and is standing behind the stage. The crowd is in a frenzy, screaming for the inevitable encore. She is making them wait and she is frozen in place, her fingers knit on the crown of her head and her elbows flared like wings. It's the posture of a runner at the end of a marathon, a way to open up starved lungs for a drink of pure air. She looks dazed, she looks happy, she looks like she might just lift off into the night sky if not for the low ceiling, the apartments above, and the simple facts of matter and gravity.

Outtakes: Var. boxes, var. spools.

KAT: What does this look like to you?

ME: Yuck. What is that?

KAT: I know, right?

ME: How long has it been like that?

KAT: I don't know. I just noticed it.

ME: You should get that looked at.

KAT: I am getting it looked at. By you.

KAT: (singing) "Woke up, fell out of bed, dragged a comb across my"—shit, are we really out of coffee?

KAT: Not now, okay? Please? Can't you just—seriously. Stop it with the camera, okay? Stop it. Cut it OUT! Why can't you just be my friend instead of a goddamn—

Interior. Evergreen Avenue loft. Kat, backlit by windows, scissors the sleeves off a T-shirt.

People will say, Isn't that wild that you two *knew* each other in high school? What are the odds? As if Kat becoming famous and me receiving some degree of—what? Highly focused niche acclaim?—were independent of each other, like lightning striking the same place twice or sisters winning the lottery within a week of each other. But the truth is simpler than any of that: Kat became Kat because her talent fit the new tastes and her personality made her catnip for a certain breed of music fan. If she was cast as the Red Queen of post-punk pop, I was her court painter. But if we were monarch and courtier, we were also model and artist. People who know me only for my photos of Kat talk about her like she was my life's work when she was only my first subject. If I was lucky to have a subject who became famous, even notorious, then Kat was lucky too: lucky to have someone get it all down on film, to create a public memory of who she was every step of the way.

And there's this, which gets overlooked: The pictures aren't good only because Kat is in them; they're good because I took them. She was perfecting her art while I was perfecting mine.

Interior. West Randolph Street condo. Kat's face in profile against a black-and-white-tile floor.

Someone at the party called me. Someone who knew that Kat had a roommate who might be able to put her back together and get her home, though I don't think getting her home was as much of a priority as getting her out of where she was—*where* in this case being the gut-rehabbed third floor of a former slaughterhouse west of the Loop, a place owned by a guy who called himself a club promoter, which meant he had access to enough drugs and high-end sound equipment to turn any room into a party. This was when Kat was losing a lot of friends. This was when Kat was making worse decisions than usual. This was when Kat had started going places without me.

I rang the buzzer and the alleged club promoter pointed to a door and he didn't say *Hi* or *Thanks so much for coming* or *We're really worried about her;* he just said, "In there." And in there was nothing I hadn't seen before, though maybe a little worse. She had one arm draped across the back of the bowl and she was trying and failing to keep her hair out of her face. She had already puked a ton. I flushed the toilet, which Kat hadn't had the will or the ability to do, and she startled as the water roared in her ear. She looked at me through the sweaty fringe of her hair. I thought she was going to say my name but she just said "So sick" over and over again like it was her mantra. She retched and threw up, retched and spit out a little more. She looked up at me again through her bangs, and her eyes were rolling in her head. She seemed like she was trying to focus. If I had been a good friend or any kind of friend, I would have held her hair and stroked her arm. I would have put a cool washcloth on her forehead and told her that it was going to be all right. I would have kept flushing with each heave and not let the bowl fill up with a night's worth of casual poisoning. But instead I swung out my Leica—a bulletproof camera, the one they use in war zones—and started shooting. I got her leaning on the toilet bowl like a pillow. I got her with the stuff pouring out of her like tar. I got her lying on the cool floor, the frazzled burr of her head against the smooth solid base of the bowl.

Contact sheet. Twenty-four-exposure study of an Econoline van during load-out. Location unknown/forgotten.
You should do a book, someone said. You should put them all together so people can see what she was like, before. And I could. I have thousands of pictures. Each one different. Each one telling the same story.

Kat on her first night as a blonde — her first night looking the way that most people remember her, the way she looks on the cover of the first album, with her bleached hair and black jeans spray-painted on her skeleton's legs.

Kat getting the thorn-wrapped heart tattooed at the nape of her neck, the one that she'd rub with her index finger when she was deep in thought, or bored, or distracted, or nursing some grudge.

Kat in that ridiculous ski hat she used to wear — pom-pom on top and earflaps down both sides of her head. She is tottering toward me on an icy sidewalk with her arms spread wide and her lips puckered like she's about to plant a big wet kiss on my face, or on the lens.

Kat at Montrose Harbor in the bright sun with the sky so clear you could put your fist through it. It was late fall and the wind was tearing at her hair and beyond her you can see whitecaps and closer to her the lake is hurling itself against the rocks, and in the middle of all this motion and light Kat looks so. Goddamn. Tired.

This is my fear: That it would be like watching a whole carousel of slides from your neighbor's trip to the Grand Canyon. You'd ooh and aah for the first five pictures or so, but there would be another ninety on the way. Somewhere in the middle, you'd stop caring, and before you reached the end, you'd hate your neighbors, hate the Grand Canyon, hate the entire Eastman Kodak corporation. None of this is going to make her more real for you. And none of it is going to bring her back.

Interior. ICU. Northwestern Memorial Hospital. Close-up of Kat's hand cupping three pills: pale blue, dull yellow, off-white.

No one agrees with me, but her last album was her best. Most people stopped paying attention during her years in LA. They got tired of watching her push it too far, they said the music was never as good as those first two albums, and they all wondered why she didn't just get it over with and die already. Instead she came back to Chicago and after lying low for a while, she put out an album with a small indie label run by guys too young to have been burned by her on her way up. I imagine that recording it, playing all the instruments herself and knitting the tracks together, must have been like those long airless days in her parents' basement. I say *imagine* because I wasn't there. I abandoned Chicago shortly after Kat left town. I had planned on sticking around and being smug about how I was keeping it real, 312-style, but when I saw my chance to go east, I went. By the time I came back to see her, after months of promises and see-you-soon messages, she was sick and then she was gone. Anyone who had guessed overdose or razor to the wrist or self-immolation must have felt cheated. She got a stupid cancer, one that had nothing to do with any of her more toxic habits, and that was it. Right before her body betrayed her that one last time, she was tiny and bald and her skin was like cigarette paper. I wanted to scoop her up and carry her back to our old loft, to the couch where we had curled up all those years before watching reruns of *Cheers* and *M*A*S*H* and *Mary Tyler Moore* and everything else WGN threw at us. Kat had fallen asleep on my shoulder that night. I listened to her breathe. I watched her dreaming eyes twitch. Her face was soft and full, despite the bruise that painted her left eye. Seeing her in that hospital bed, that's what I wanted: to carry her back home.

THAT'S WHAT WOULD happen in the dream sequence where the best friends are reunited after the falling-out, the bitter words, the long silence, the gradual thaw. But I did not spirit her away. When I found her in that bed, wiped out and with little left to give, I aimed the lens and started to shoot. Because not getting those pictures would have wrecked it—for me. And, I hope, for her.

Looking at all of the pictures now, I can pretend that she was the only one with the *What the fuck?* look, the *What makes you so special?* look, the *Do you even believe your own bullshit?* look. But she's also the only one with the *Thank God it's you* look, the *Just trust me on this one* look, the *I'm sorry, please forgive me* look, the *Look that I only give to you* look. This is when I wish that there had been another me as devoted to me as I was to her. Someone to offer me proof that I looked at her like that instead of just gawking with one big glassy eye that only asked for more, and more, and more, and more.

Airborne

Jenna tells Dan he's crazy. He's home from work for five minutes, his tie is still knotted, and already he's nosing around the central-air vents and the drains, inside the cabinets and behind the refrigerator. He hasn't even said hello to Lucy, their three-year-old. Instead he's sniffing the fireplace and the showerheads. He drops to his knees to check the carpet in the den. He stomps down the stairs to the basement. He pokes his head into the attic.

It's the mold again. He says it's so bad he can smell it, and that's when Jenna tells him he's crazy. The cleaning ladies were at the house all afternoon, and the place is awash in lemon-scented floor wax and furniture polish, spiked with the tang of Windex and bleach. Jenna believes that this cocktail of scrubs, cleansers, waxes, and sprays has a mood-enhancing effect stronger than Prozac, which she has never tried, but weaker than Ecstasy, which she has. Colors seem brighter, shapes more distinct, as if the house sits on a mountaintop in the Alps instead of at the end of a cul-de-sac in Wilmette. She tells Dan they pay good money for the house to smell like this.

"You're used to it," he says. "If you spent all day out of the house, you'd notice it the second you came in."

"I'm going to pretend you didn't say that," she says. "For your sake, I'm going to pretend you didn't say a word." In the two years since Jenna quit her job as assistant vice president of packaging for a specialty foods company to stay home with Lucy, she has heard him pose this question more times and in more ways than she can count: *Just what is it that you do all day?*

"Don't be that way," he says. "You know what I mean."

"Yeah," she says. "I know exactly what you mean."

DAN IS AT work, brainstorming ways to position foil-wrapped cheese sticks as an extreme snack food for preteen skateboarders. Lucy is at preschool, sprinkling glitter on paper plates smeared with glue. Jenna has the house to herself. There is a long list of things that she should be doing: *laundry (Lucy's/ours), repot zinnias, supermarket (don't forget list), dry cleaning, buy lightbulbs (lots!), call Ruth Ann re: playdate.* But the house is quiet and clean, and Jenna drifts from room to room, her second cup of coffee faintly steaming in her hand. She wants to enjoy these stolen moments—moments that she never includes on any to-do list (*wander aimlessly in the house, flip through back issues of food magazines*)—but instead she catches herself in the hallway pausing to sniff the air. She leans into Lucy's room, sniffs again. There's nothing; honestly, nothing.

It started a few weeks ago. Lucy was asleep, the glasses were clinking in the dishwasher, and Dan and Jenna were in the living room. Dan was hunched over his laptop, tweaking storyboards for a client pitch the next morning. Jenna sat next to him on the couch, halfway through her book club's latest selection—a novel by a long-dead Nobel laureate with a consonant-stuffed Scandinavian name. Jenna would have quit the book a hundred pages ago and faked her way through the discussion, but she had recommended it to the group without having read it and felt obliged to slog to the end. On the television, a documentary about polar exploration was in its final minutes. Scott and Amundsen were racing to the South Pole. Scott and his party had opted for ponies instead of sled dogs to carry their gear. The narrator called this *a fateful decision.*

"I think we would have gone with the ponies too," Jenna said without lowering her book. "I mean, if we'd let Lucy make the decision. Definitely ponies."

Dan yanked a tissue from the box next to the couch and blew his nose. "Ponies are good," he said, his eyes fixed on the computer screen. "And if it gets too cold, you can cut them open and crawl inside while they're still warm." Dan dabbed his nose with the tissue.

"Yuck," Jenna said. "Lucy would definitely not let you do that."

"Like in *Empire Strikes Back,*" he said. "That was some kind of two-legged outer-space snow camel, but in an emergency? I'd do it."

The narrator read from Scott's journal, describing how they shot the weakened ponies and packed the meat for the return trip. "Yuck again," Jenna said. "What is it with you men and killing ponies?"

"Maybe the ponies got hungry too," he said. "It was eat or be eaten." Dan blew his nose again. "Look at this." The wadded tissue was spotted with blood.

She glanced at the tissue and winced. "I'd hate to see the other guy," she said.

Dan tilted his head back and pinched his nostrils shut. "Very funny," he said. On the screen, actors portraying Scott and his exhausted companions reached the South Pole—only to find a riot of dog tracks, a Norwegian flag, and a note from Amundsen.

"Sorry old chap," Jenna said. "Beat you to it. Enjoy the walk back home."

"Hey," Dan said. "I'm bleeding over here." He groped for the box and began wadding tissues into his nostrils.

"You want some ice?" She said it absently, her book still open, because, really, it was just a little blood.

"What am I supposed to do? Stick the cubes up my nose?"

Jenna closed her book. Too many nights lately had shifted on the axis of a careless word or a joke that came out sharper than intended. She didn't want this to be one of those nights. Jenna aimed the remote control at the television and flicked the off button; the rescue party had found the frozen bodies of Scott and his companions only miles from base camp. "So tell me," she said, turning toward Dan and folding her legs beneath her, "what happened to your nose?"

"Nothing happened," he said. "It just started bleeding."

He was breathing through his mouth; his nose was inflated

with tissues and his jaw hung open, slack. He looked like a movie thug, like someone else's Dan. She took his face in her hands, feeling the stubble on his cheeks. He had nicked himself shaving, right in the middle of his chin, though she hadn't noticed in the morning when the cut was fresh. His hair was getting long—or maybe he was letting it grow to cover the retreat of his hairline or to mimic some new style. She wasn't sure; they didn't talk much about his hair. They talked about his job, the house, Lucy. They could go whole days talking only about Lucy: what she said, how much she ate, how often she used the potty.

Dan's breathing slowed. Jenna wondered how long it had been since they had stared at each other like this, face-to-face. *Look deep into my eyes,* she almost said in her best movie-hypnotist voice.

"I think it's the house," Dan said.

"What's the house?" she said.

"That's making my nose bleed," he said.

Jenna pulled her hands from his face. Not this again.

He inhaled sharply, his teeth parted and his tongue cupping the air, as if he were tasting a glass of wine. "Don't you feel that?" he said. "There's something in the air."

"Don't start, okay?"

"I'm serious," he said. "I think there's something wrong with the house."

Jenna tried to ignore him—to actively, silently ignore him. They had endured two years of rooms sealed off by sheets of heavy plastic while subcontractors scraped, sanded, drywalled, and painted; two years that Jenna had spent restoring and refinishing, stenciling and papering. The work was done (finally) and the house felt like home (finally!) instead of a construction site where they were furtively squatting. But Dan kept finding faults—the dimmer switch she'd chosen was a dial instead of a sliding bar, the stain Jenna had used on the mantel was Early American Cherry and not Colonial Maple, and now this: the house was giving him a nosebleed.

Dan inhaled again, two deep, doctor's-office breaths. "There's definitely something," he said, sitting up straight and turning away from Jenna. "I can't believe you don't feel it."

Jenna couldn't feel anything, then or now, but Dan wouldn't let it go. A few days after his nosebleed he saw a report about mold on the news, or he read about it in a magazine, or he saw it online—"As if it matters," he said when Jenna pressed him about his source. He was convinced that somewhere in the house spores were flourishing, and a day hadn't passed without some new manifestation of the blight: another nosebleed, a headache, a tightness in his chest, and, most recently, the smell.

HE WAKES JENNA in the middle of the night. "Lucy's coughing," he says. The sound pulses in the hallway, a wet cough that bursts like a punch in the stomach. "She's been coughing all night."

"Flu season," Jenna says, burrowing into her pillow. "There's a bug going around her class." They are close enough to touch, if either of them wants to.

"You know it's the mold," he says.

"She's in preschool," Jenna says. "She'll probably be sick until April."

"There was a thing about it on the news again tonight."

"Dan, we don't have toxic mold. We have a daughter with a cold."

He rolls onto his side, jerking the sheets, his face to the wall. "If you say so," he says. There's a lot more that Jenna could say, but it's three in the morning and Lucy will be awake in a few hours, so she doesn't say the thing that's been nagging at her for weeks: that the house was Dan's idea.

Before Lucy, their lives fit neatly into a nine-hundred-square-foot West Loop condo with an open floor plan and a third-floor balcony. Then they had Lucy, and the balcony with its wide-spaced rails, the bars serving four-ingredient cocktails, the restaurants where every table was a two-top—everything about their old life seemed not simply inadequate but selfish, even dangerous. By the time Lucy started taking her first wobbly steps, Dan was talking up the virtues of homeownership: no neighbors stomping unseen on the floor above, no late-night ambulances and idling garbage trucks in the street below, and a yard where Lucy could play while Jenna tended a garden. Hadn't Jenna always wanted to take up gardening?

Lying in the dark, with Lucy's cough battering the bedroom door, Jenna still can't answer that question. When she weighs her old life against this one, she can admit to missing certain things. But no matter how much she tots up in favor of the old life, it always comes down to a simple question, a question she can answer: Would you trade Lucy to have all of that back?

The next morning, when Jenna tells Dan that she's keeping Lucy home from school for the day because of her cough, he asks if that's really the best thing for her. "She's probably safer at school," he says. "Being here is only going to prolong her exposure."

"Her exposure to what?" Jenna says.

"Forget it," he says, but that night he comes home from work with an air purifier as big as a beer keg. He tells Jenna that the IoMatic is the top of the line for in-home air quality, with a filter that received an A-plus rating for mold spores, dander, dust mites, pollen, you name it. He tells her their air will be so clean that they will be able to taste the difference. So clean it will make them giddy, like breathing pure oxygen. She knows he is repeating verbatim what the salesman told him. He is pitching her, as if she were a client shopping an account; as if this barrel-size machine were going to make her smile whiter, her hair more lustrous.

"Nothing gets past this baby," Dan says, patting the box with a dog-show handler's mix of affection and desperate hope. He spouts more salesman talk about how the IoMatic electrically charges the air, how it traps foreign particles in the easy-clean filter.

"It electrifies the air?" Jenna says, halting him mid-patter. "That sounds dangerous."

"Not electrify; electrically charge." Now it's Dan who sounds exasperated, as if he's trying to explain to Lucy for the hundredth time why she can't wear her rain boots to bed. He starts to say something about verification and laboratories and independent analysis, but Jenna stops listening and climbs the stairs to tell Lucy that Daddy is home and it's time to come down for dinner.

After two nights of the IoMatic inhaling 99.7 percent of harmful household allergens, Lucy is still coughing. Jenna doesn't taste anything new in the air. She is not giddy.

JENNA IS SHOPPING for lightbulbs at the home-improvement superstore. They seem to go through a lot of lightbulbs, and she wonders if Dan blames this on the mold too. Boxes containing chandeliers, patio furniture, and lawn mowers are stacked on shelves three stories high. It wasn't long ago that Jenna could tell from fifty feet away which companies were using four-color digital printers for their packaging and which used a six-color offset press; which boxes were laminated and therefore practically unrecyclable and which had some percentage of postconsumer waste. She could have priced in her head the cost, with volume discounts, of ordering one hundred thousand units, half a million, a million. It was second nature. But now, with the orange metal joists and the white corrugated ceiling looming above her, all she feels is dizzy. Everything about the store seems magnified, dangerously out of scale, as if she is at the top of the beanstalk. Down one of these aisles, there is a goose that lays golden eggs. Down another, a hungry giant sleeps.

As she counts the numbered signs at the end of each aisle, she notices a man standing near a row of sugar-white washing machines. He looks like he is trying to remember where he left his keys, but something about him—the way his head swivels and darts, the way he lifts himself on the balls of his feet and cranes his neck—tells her that his confusion masks a growing panic. The man stops one of the orange-vested employees and holds his hands out in front of him, as if he has just dropped something heavy but can't for the life of him remember when or where. One hand clutches a child's empty baseball cap. The employee nods and sets his mouth in a grim line and Jenna hears him loud and clear when he raises the walkie-talkie to his mouth and barks, "Code Adam, we've got a Code Adam."

Jenna feels a knot in her stomach, a polyp of dread that doubles when she looks at her own hands and realizes that they too are empty. She should be cradling the delicate bird-body of Lucy's hand, but instead her hands hang limp and useless at her sides. Like the man by the washing machines, she swivels and darts her head and the dread bursts, drenching her in fear and sweat—just as she remembers that she came alone. Lucy is home, finger-painting or pushing her wooden circus train across the couch or begging her father for one more sing-along video.

She lets out a long breath, exhaling fumes of acid terror. She raises her eyes to the thin skin of ribbed metal spread out high above her. In the department that sells doors and windows, she finds the same orange-vested employee, a man whose name tag is three inked capital letters: RED. She wants to ask if they've found the child, but instead she asks where the bathroom is, and when she finds it, she locks the door and breathes raggedly for five minutes, trying to keep herself from crying.

She does not tell Dan. Not about the crying or the man with the empty baseball cap or RED or the Code Adam or the lost boy, whom she saw sobbing next to his father at the customer-service counter. She never tells him about the newspapers, either. Jenna still picks up the folded newspaper from the front porch every morning and leaves it on the kitchen table where Dan will read it as he eats his breakfast, but she hasn't looked at the paper in months. She knows that the pages crawl with colonies of black type seething about gunmen and hit-and-runs, chatter and sleepers and Amber Alerts. She knows that a single word or picture can conjure visions of disaster—Lucy hurt, Lucy missing, Lucy's body found—that she will spend the rest of the day trying to dispel. So she waits for Dan to eat and read and leave for work, and then she carries the paper like a soiled rag to the recycling bin in the garage.

JENNA PUTS LUCY down for the night. Lucy sleeps in a big-girl bed with padded rails on each side. Jenna often curls up with Lucy after she reads her a bedtime story; she says it's to help Lucy fall asleep, but she suspects that she needs those few minutes more than Lucy does. She drapes an arm around Lucy's tiny shoulders and inhales the sweet, soapy scent of her hair. A fan churns on top of the bookcase, dampening the sounds of the house at night—the dishwasher being loaded, the television in the living room, the heat clicking on and off in response to the thermostat's orders. As on most nights, Jenna falls asleep in Lucy's bed, waking with a start to find Lucy pressed between her body and the rail. She kisses Lucy's forehead and lifts herself out of the bed, her movements slow and wistful.

She finds Dan in the dining room, his ear pressed to the wall. "So now you can hear it?" she says, trying to sound amused but knowing that she's coming across as mocking, even bitchy.

He is startled, and as he stands up he almost stumbles into

the sprawling checkerboard of wall-mounted shadow boxes that houses Jenna's teapot collection. The first gift Dan ever bought her was a teapot—the story behind it, which she once considered sweetly romantic, was now simply too long to tell—and during the years that followed she had built the collection by trolling through antique stores, flea markets, and junk shops. She had the case custom built for the best pieces in her collection, a mix of stoneware, pottery, china, and enamelware, and had it remounted after the move. There are times when Jenna is alone in the house and she feels she is seeing the collection for the first time in all of its meticulously chosen glory and all she can think is: *What a waste.* She tries to tally up all of the time and money spent, and for what? Teapots? In the city, part of their charm was the way they existed not as functional objects—as pots for making tea—but as little works of art that didn't have to do anything to be valuable. But here she can't stop herself from thinking, *What am I going to do with all of these teapots? I don't even like tea.*

Dan runs his hand over the wall as if there's a wrinkle in the paint that can be smoothed. "It could be anywhere," he says.

"Or," she says, "it could be nowhere."

"What's it going to take?" he says. "You want us all in the hospital?"

"No one's going to the hosp—"

"Jenna!" he says. Lately it seems that Dan begins a lot of his sentences in the same teeth-gritted way: *Jenna!* He starts to tell her about black mold, white mold, orange mold, green mold. For every color of the rainbow, a mold. There's a mold that causes rashes, a mold that causes asthma, a mold that causes memory loss, a mold that can kill you. She tells him that the only mold she has ever seen in the house was on a wedge of Brie in the refrigerator.

He turns his head and presses his other ear to the wall. He sneezes once, explosively, into his hands.

"Did you hear that?" he says.

"The mold?" Jenna says, and immediately she knows that tonight they will sleep as far from each other as the queen-size bed allows.

"No, not the mold." he says. "Just being this close to the wall is enough to make you sneeze."

"No," she says. "It's enough to make *you* sneeze."

"And what about Lucy?" he says. "Do you still say it's the flu?"

"Don't bring her into this," she says. "If you want to go crazy, fine. But you're going there on your own."

Jenna waits, engine idling, to pick up Lucy at preschool. There are at least a dozen vehicles in the line, but hers is the only station wagon among the humped roofs and fanged grilles of the minivans and SUVs. It's a Volvo, but still she wonders if she has somehow broken one of the rules that govern how, when, and by whom the children are to be dropped off and picked up. Perhaps an addendum to the parents' handbook was sent home with the children one day, a single sheet of colored paper that Lucy lost, or Jenna ignored, that specified the makes and models of automobiles that would safely convey children to and from the school's pleasant, architect-designed doors.

She's early today and waits in line to approach the Pickup Point. When her turn comes, one of the teachers will lift Lucy into her car seat, and then Jenna will slowly roll forward into the Buckle-Up Zone. Only here can Jenna get out of the car and clip Lucy into her car seat—clipping in at the Pickup Point slows things down for everyone and is frowned upon. Although it's only fifty feet from the point to the zone, Jenna always feels a rush, a transgressive charge that reminds her of shoplifting, as she drives at five miles an hour while Lucy rides in back untethered.

As she sits, she watches airplanes paint contrails across the sky. Before Lucy was born, she and Dan always held hands during takeoff. Their fingers would seek each other out and twine while with their other hands they flipped through magazines or balanced the spines of paperbacks. In that hiccup of weightlessness when the wheels lost contact with the runway, she would feel a sudden squeeze from him, and she would squeeze back. It was an unspoken contract, this squeezing of hands, and it sent a placid certainty flooding through her. She would look at his face in profile, his eyes scanning the slick bright pages of a magazine, and she would think: *I am exactly where I want to be right now. Even if this plane goes down, I am where I most want to be.*

The first time they flew with Lucy, Jenna put her next to the window so she could watch the bags being loaded into the rib cage of the plane. Lucy stood on her seat, pointing at each bag as it trundled up the belt: "I see a red one! I see a black one! I see a black one! I see a black one!" Later, as the plane accelerated down the runway and the fuselage thrummed and the tray tables rattled against their pegs, Jenna reached for Lucy's hand. It was tiny inside hers. Lights flickered past the oval window, the interval between each blue flash shrinking as they neared take-off. Lucy turned to her, her eyes wide. "Mommy, we're flying! We're flying!" And as the wheels lifted, Jenna saw the plane not as an object made and controlled by human beings with specialized knowledge but as a stone launched from a slingshot. She gripped her daughter's hand—her fingers, her palm, her wrist—but even so, she felt hollowed out, empty; she was the broken eggshell trying to keep her golden yolk from slipping away.

A car horn sounds—a gentle prod—and Jenna realizes that it's her turn at the Pickup Point. Lucy is standing at the curb, holding hands with her teacher, their arms swinging in a carefree arc. As the teacher lifts Lucy into the padded embrace of her car seat, she says, "We had a little accident today," and hands Jenna a white plastic bag that Jenna knows from experience contains a soiled pair of underpants, wrapped as neatly as restaurant leftovers.

DAN HAS SCHEDULED an inspection. He tells Jenna that they should check into a hotel until they get the report. Of course she refuses. She is willing to go along with the inspection, but she wants that to be the end of it.

"The end?" he says. "It could be the beginning. It all depends on what they find." He goes into detail about the possibilities: *Penicillium, Aspergillus,* the dreaded *Stachybotrys.* His vocabulary has become more advanced; the list of harmful effects exponentially longer. He uses the word *mycotoxins*. He mentions the need for microbial volatile organic compound analysis. He tells her about rothounds, dogs trained in Denmark to sniff out dry rot.

"You're bringing in dogs?" she says. They are standing in the kitchen on either side of an island topped by granite as dark and smooth as black ice. Above the island, copper pots hang from a rack that Jenna mounted on the ceiling using a cordless drill she bought at the superstore.

"Whatever it takes," he says.

"Whatever it takes to do what?"

"To get to the bottom of this." He says it like it's the obvious answer, the only answer. He takes a deep breath, his eyes fixed on the polished pots and skillets. He once complained that the pots hung too low, too close to his line of vision, and Jenna can't help wondering if he is thinking about this right now.

"I'm doing this for you," he says. "For you and Lucy."

"Well, don't." The words burst out of her. "Please don't." The man on the other side of the kitchen island doesn't even look like Dan—not really—but she tries to tell herself that this is something Dan does: He throws himself headlong into everything. It is some fundamental part of who he is—even something she loves about him. Years before, when they first moved in together, he was put in charge of a campaign for a new bottled water from Germany. For the next month, everything he had once done with water, he instead did with Wøder. She found him one morning in the bathroom, emptying three cases of luke-warm Wøder into the tub. On the bath mat, an enormous black garbage bag bulged with empties. "I should have told them to send the liter bottles," he said. "Twelve ounces at a time is killing me." During that whole month, Dan—that Dan—never complained when she took a shower or ran the dishwasher or drank a glass of plain old water.

"Can't we just agree," she says, "that everything's okay?"

"Okay?" he says. "This is real, Jenna. It's real and it's all around us."

"It's not around us," she says, and she stabs one finger at him. "It's in your stupid fucking head."

"You're right," Dan says. "It's in my head and my lungs and my blood and God knows where else." He grips the granite edge of the island and leans forward, closing the gap between them. "It's in me and it's in you and it's in Lucy. That's what I've been trying to tell you."

"Stop saying that about her," Jenna says. "Stop acting like you're the only one who cares, or so help me—"

"Of course you care," he says. "Look, I never—" He pauses, shakes his head. "Let's just get the inspection. Then we'll know."

"I already know," she says.

"You don't," he says. "You said so yourself. You just want us to agree that we know."

"And what do you want?"

"I want to get to the bottom of it," he says.

Dan wants to get to the bottom of it, but Jenna knows now that there is no bottom. If the inspectors turn the house inside out and can't find a single speck of mold, that won't be the bottom. And if there's a velvety scrim of *Stachy*-this and *Asper*-that behind every wall, that won't be the bottom either. She knows now that it can always go deeper.

JENNA PICKS UP Lucy at preschool and takes her to the park for a picnic. This is exactly the sort of thing that all of the parenting magazines recommend—special mommy-daughter time, a break from the daily routine—but Jenna knows that her motives for staying out of the house are not entirely pure. Since the inspection last week, the house feels agitated, like a snow globe that hasn't yet settled. Or maybe it's Jenna who feels the flutter and drift of being shaken. The inspectors came, armed with handheld meters and long drill bits. They spoke of swabs and core samples. They wore masks and latex gloves. The rothounds were lean and serious—they were dogs, not doggies—and with their noses to the baseboards, they traced the perimeter of every room and hallway. The preliminary report had come back clean, but there were still air samples to be analyzed, patches of drywall to be tested.

At the park, Lucy scoops wood chips with a plastic cup while two older girls shimmy their hula hoops into motion. There are beads inside each hoop, and with every revolution, they chatter and buzz. The way the hoops spin activates some vestigial part of Jenna's brain that sees a circle and thinks of pie charts, market share, and PowerPoint slides. She thinks how she and Dan were once like two overlapping circles, a Venn diagram of autonomous crescents and a common oval that held the best part of each of them. Now they are as jagged as gears, each working against the natural motion of the other. On each hand, she touches the index finger to the thumb and considers the two loops.

"Mommy, look," Lucy says. She has shaped her hands in imitation of her mother's and holds them up to her eyes. "It's my min-oc-lee-ers. I see you, Mommy!"

Jenna brings her curled fingers up to her eyes. "I see you too, sweetheart."

Lucy scans the playground. "I spy a slide," she says. This is how she plays I Spy. Instead of providing a clue—"I spy something red"—she names the thing she sees.

Jenna follows Lucy's gaze, still locked on the slide. "There it is!" she says.

Lucy squeals with delight and tells Jenna that it's her turn to spy something, so Jenna cranes her neck, her face tilted to the sky. "I spy something white and puffy."

Lucy shrieks. "Clouds!" she says. They go back and forth—"I spy two girls"; "I spy something green and full of leaves"—until Lucy uncurls her fingers and starts sorting the mulched wood chips into two buckets, one for the nice wood and the other for the mean wood. Jenna keeps her handmade binoculars up to her eyes and aims them at Lucy. The park is shuttered behind her fingers; her daughter fills her field of vision. She wants to look at Lucy with such intensity that she burns an image of her daughter into the backs of her eyes: the curve of her ear, the swell of her cheeks, the color of her eyes, every curl on her head. When Jenna finally removes her hands, she is startled by how big and bright the world seems. The sky is a pool of pulsing neon. The autumn leaves are as vibrant as sea coral. Children race across the grass in jackets that glow like hard candy.

Driving home from the park, Jenna negotiates the fretwork

of speed bumps on their street. She sees Dan's car in the driveway—Dan, who is rarely home before six—and the sour realization settles over her that she won't have the quiet hours of Lucy's afternoon nap all to herself. After she parks and unsnaps the restraints on the car seat, Lucy bounds into the driveway, resuming the words to a song that Jenna does not know.

The door is unlocked, and Jenna calls Dan's name as she enters the house. On the table in the foyer she sees his splayed keys and a large white envelope, ripped open across the top. The inspection company's logo is in one corner and Dan's office address is printed at the center. She calls Dan's name again, and from the back of the house she hears a thud and a rattle, like crushed ice pouring from the dispenser on the refrigerator, only much louder. She tells Lucy to stay by the door.

In the dining room she finds Dan ripping through the drywall with a crowbar. Two of the teapots have fallen and shattered; she sees busted handles, broken spouts. Each time the crowbar bites into the wall, the other teapots quiver and clink in their case. They are skewed, off-center. Some are teetering on the edge. She pauses for a moment, waiting for the next blow and hoping that another of the pots will fall. The dining-room floor—its delicately painted surface, its carefully stenciled border—is under a gritty film of crushed gypsum. Jagged chunks of drywall lean against the baseboards.

"They couldn't find it," Dan says, stricken. The tie that Jenna gave him for his birthday, the shirt she bought him because it made his eyes sparkle, the shoes she convinced him to splurge on because good shoes matter—all of it is coated in gray dust. Dan looks down at the crowbar in his hands as if he's calculating the weight of it, then swings it into the breach he has already torn. The curved end bites into the drywall, and he yanks it once, twice, a third time before it pulls free another chunk.

"Dan," she says, and the word comes out more softly than she'd intended. She reaches out one hand and says his name again. He is breathing hard, his face streaked with grit and sweat. She knows that he is doing this for her and Lucy. She also knows that he is doing it for himself. He needs this, and she hopes that this alone will be enough. She crosses the room, both hands in front of her, the way she would approach a cornered stray. She wants to tell him that it's all going to be okay, that it's over now, but she can't bring herself to say what she doesn't believe. So she takes him in her arms and she feels his weight. She feels him gripping her shoulder like he's hanging from a ledge. And as she takes a deep breath, she feels against her ribs the hard edge of the crowbar, still fast in his hand.

How Long Does
the First Part Last?

He thinks about ardor and the Virginia state line.

His college roommate Webb once drove from North Carolina to New York City with Rachel, the object of a four-year unspoken crush—a woman already engaged to a bow-tied investment banker who hadn't taken one single English class during his four years in Chapel Hill. One hour into the trip, just as they crossed into Virginia, he poured his heart out to her in a monologue that started with the first moment he saw her: freshman year, discreetly transferring her underwear from a dryer into a laundry basket in the dorm basement. Webb offered a confession of anonymous kindnesses and secret devotions: he had once tied a red ribbon, a symbol of his ardor—that's exactly the word he used when he told the story, *ardor*—to the handlebars of her bicycle. He had a fallen leaf she had handed him sophomore year pressed between the onionskin pages of his *Norton Anthology of English Literature,* volume 1. He told her that on the night during their junior year that it had snowed six inches, snowflakes had collected like stars in her eyelashes, and every time he thought about it his heart broke wide open. He concluded by telling her, "I need you to know that I love you."

Rachel sat stiffly, her eyes on the corridor of pines that picketed the interstate. She took a single shallow breath and said, "I don't feel the same way."

They drove the next eight hours without speaking. When he returned to Chapel Hill, Webb stayed drunk for three days, after which he announced that he was over her, which he wasn't.

HE THINKS ABOUT choices and the cardboard man.

His friend Sylvie had come into possession of a life-size cardboard cutout of a comedian she didn't recognize promoting a movie she had never seen. She found it in the storage room of the two-screen theater where she worked, took it back to her apartment, and named it Donald, after the perpetual boyfriend in *That Girl*. Sylvie propped him up in the kitchen and talked to him over breakfast. She stood him in the living room when she had friends over for drinks.

"Donald is a people person," she said, and most of her guests agreed that Donald seemed to perk up in a crowd. If he wasn't much of a conversationalist, he was an excellent listener.

Donald spent most of his time in Sylvie's bedroom, where he could advise her on clothing choices and keep a watchful eye on her while she slept. Because Donald was giving a thumbs-up, some people thought he was a pushover, but Sylvie swore that the thumb would waver when he thought sandals were a bad idea or if her boot-cuts looked a little too bell-bottom.

The only person who didn't like Donald was Sylvie's boyfriend. He was tired of the way Sylvie asked Donald where he thought they should go to dinner or what he wanted to watch on TV. He said it was just a way for Sylvie to get another vote. But what really got to him was Donald being in Sylvie's bedroom. He said it was creepy having Donald there when they slept together, and he accused Sylvie of fantasizing about a three-way with him and Donald whenever they had sex. The truth was, Sylvie had started to fantasize about sex with Donald only. The boyfriend was just there for the breath and the muscle.

One night they came home drunk from a party and collapsed on the bed, where they started the electric, clumsy business of undressing each other. The boyfriend was down to his briefs—an underwear choice that Donald never would have made—when he bolted from the bed.

"I want this thing out of here!" He swiped at Donald and tore off his thumbs-up hand. For emphasis, he threw the hand out the second-story window. He cocked his arm to throw a punch at Donald's toothy grin, but Sylvie leaped between them. Her hair was a wild mess, and she clutched a sheet to her chest. She pointed at the window, her arm rigid.

"You get his hand right now!"

"His?" The boyfriend shoved Donald but couldn't knock him off balance. "It's a piece of cardboard! It's a goddamn picture!"

"Now!" she said.

"Are you kidding me?" he said, and from her face he knew

that she wasn't. "Look, it's me or Donald. Because you can't have both."

"Fine," she said. "I pick Donald."

He stared, slack-jawed and still drunk, for a full ten seconds before he started gathering up his clothes and muttering loudly about how crazy she was and what bullshit this was and how he had put up with it for long enough.

In the morning Sylvie retrieved Donald's hand from the bushes below her window and reattached it with a stapler and Scotch tape. She said she never regretted dumping the boyfriend. She said she wished that every decision in life was that straight-forward, that clear-cut.

HE THINKS ABOUT freight trains and the steepest stretches of I-40.

"Can we not talk," she said.

They had been driving for two hours and it was the first thing Karen had said since leaving her parents' cabin in Saluda. Two hours of the mountains rising and falling, never rising as sharply as the time before, until the Appalachians just gave up and stumbled into the Piedmont. He had kept his eyes on the road the whole time, waiting for her to say something. When after two hours she still hadn't and he said, without looking at her, "I just think we should——" she didn't even turn away from the passenger-side window, she just said, "Can we not talk." It wasn't a request or a plea; it was the answer to the question that had been stalking him for months, and now it had him, and he didn't fight it.

The car radio was busted and a mixtape played in a boom

box in the backseat. The boom box was old and spattered with paint and when the tape ended it didn't reverse its gears and play side B. It just stopped.

He drove, and he thought about the highway just east of Asheville where on the rapid descent from the mountains, runaway-truck ramps sprouted at half-mile intervals. They weren't ramps at all, just blunt outlets that terminated in a heap of loosely packed gravel. When a trucker lost his brakes, he barreled down the highway in a riot of flashing lights and blaring horns, hustling through lanes of child-packed minivans, sedans full of elderly leaf-peepers, and church buses ferrying the faithful to Bible study. The trucker had to know that the mountain was steep and that speed would overtake even the straightest line he could hold, that sooner or later the truck would turn fatally inward and jackknife across four crowded lanes. The ramps offered a sudden end to the maddening descent, to all of the screaming and swerving; they let the driver choose the time and place for the disaster. And if the trucker was lucky or his load particularly light, he could walk away battered, dazed, but intact.

Karen wasn't wearing a seat belt, and she had her legs drawn up against her chest in a pose he had once thought of as sweet and vulnerable, but the only word that came to mind in the moment was *selfish*. If there had been a runaway-truck ramp on the flats west of Winston-Salem, he would have buried the nose of his car in the gravel and catapulted her through the windshield and out of his life. Instead he kept his foot on the gas and let the car drift, just slightly, onto the corrugated asphalt on the shoulder of the highway.

"What are you doing?" she said. She looked only mildly annoyed, as if he wasn't even worth the energy it took to get angry anymore.

"Shh," he said. "We're not talking."

They had spent the past four days not talking about the only thing left to talk about. She said the mountains would give them a better view of their lives than they could get at sea level. It was the kind of thing she said all the time; her loopy, half-sensical way with words had been one of the reasons he had fallen for her. In their early days together, everything about her had enchanted him: the patterned tights she wore in the winter; the way she danced, head bowed and arms swaying, as if she were dusting a table; even her job at the record store where she bummed cigarettes off the faculty brats and the seventh-year seniors.

Outside Saluda they hiked to the ridge overlooking the railroad right-of-way that cut through the trees and rock faces. It was the steepest grade east of the Mississippi, that's what she had told him, and when the eastbound coal trains got half of their weight on the downward slope, the engineers locked their brakes and let gravity do the rest. The trains slid down the rails, inching through the town, until the track leveled out somewhere in the foothills. It was slow going, but there wasn't really any choice: ride the brakes or wreck the town. At the spot where they watched the train there was a tall shade tree and a wrought-iron bench that had been there since the turn of the century. Watching the trains was once a popular pastime, a backdrop for picnic lunches and young lovers' rendezvous.

He wanted to believe that they could find a way around

everything that had come between them—an easily discerned path, visible from the top of the ridge. But all he had found in Saluda were photos of Karen shivering by the creek at seven, smiling through her braces at fourteen, and sticking out her tongue at some high-school boyfriend. There weren't any pictures of him in the cabin and there never would be, because as soon as the words *Can we not talk* were out of her mouth, he knew that this ride, these four hours, were the last hours that they would spend so close to each other.

It would take weeks to untangle the frayed strands that bound them together, but that work he did separately, over drinks with friends who told him it had gone on long enough, in messages he left when he knew she was not home, and in the back of a U-Haul while she was at work. And when it was over, it was over. The ache subsided faster than he'd expected it to, and when he finally took his brother up on his offer of a place to stay in Chicago, he left town without calling her. Not out of spite, but just because.

HE THINKS ABOUT all of it—about Webb and Rachel and Sylvie and Donald and Karen and the ride home from Saluda—and just how easy it was. He thinks about it when the lawyer tells him to list everything—*everything!*—whether he wants it or not. He thinks about it whenever he feels her hand in his, as real as a phantom limb. He thinks about it when the light is pulsing on the answering machine in the barely furnished apartment and there are ten messages and every one of them says *Goddamn it, you bastard, you son of a bitch.* He thinks about it twice a week as his car idles in the parking lot of a dentist's office halfway between the house and the apartment because it's the only place they can agree to meet to exchange the kids. He thinks about it during the second, smaller birthday parties and during his off weekends when he stands in the extra bedroom, staring at the cartoon faces on the bedspreads that he hoped would make this place feel like home. And he thinks about it in the summer when his younger daughter's lower lip quivers and she says, "Two weeks?" and starts crying that she wants to see Mommy. She wants Mommy now.

He wishes in these moments that he could speed through these weeks and months and let what the two of them once had and what it has become explode in a burst of glass and gravel, just for the thrill of seeing it all end and knowing it was over. But he knows there is nothing in the life he lives now that can be as sudden and final as the ramp. And he knows that what he had before Saluda, and what Webb confessed to across the Virginia state line, and what Sylvie pretended she felt for Donald—none of it was love.

He has a choice, but it is no choice at all. He waits for the long crawl to the bottom, keeping in check all of that dark mass and its potential for combustion. He waits until he can again move under his own power. And he knows that if he loses his grip or tries to rush the way it must go, then he will only spread the damage to those who least deserve it and can least bear its weight.

Dunn & Sons

This is the story my father never tells.

It is August 1973. My father, Theobald Dunn, is twenty-four. For the past three years he has been stationed at a U.S. Army base in Alaska, listening for the first stirrings of a Soviet missile launch. Before that, he spent a year studying for the priesthood at a seminary outside Boston. Before that, he attended college for three semesters. Now he is back in Wiltwyck, New York, the town where he was born and raised, working at my grandfather's hardware store.

My father's father, Patrick Dunn, is sixty. He is a naturalized citizen, a registered Republican, and the past president of the Ulster County Chamber of Commerce. He buys a new Cadillac every three years; when he trades in the old car for the new, the older car is pristine. Like the cars he buys, he has a defiantly angular appearance: chin like the grille of his '72 Fleetwood, his body a wedge of folded steel and knife-edged chrome. In four months—two weeks before Christmas—he will suffer his third heart attack, the one that finally does him in, while shoveling snow in his driveway.

His hardware store, Dunn & Sons, sits on Main Street in Wiltwyck. He named the store when his sons were still in grade school, an uncharacteristically sentimental act testifying to his faith in the future—the & Sons a promise that the generations would work hand in hand to guarantee the availability of tools, paint, and plumbing supplies in the middle Hudson Valley. My grandfather is fond of saying that he gave the boys their good looks and the names of Irish patriots to carry into the world—what they did after that was their own business. But the name of the store suggests that "their own business" already has an ad in the Yellow Pages and a team in the Wiltwyck Little League.

My grandfather has a regular tee time at Wiltwyck Country Club—Saturdays at two, just late enough for him to close the store, drink a gin and tonic in the men's grill, and change into his two-tone golf shoes. He rarely asks his sons to play with him, but that Saturday in August, he invites my father and my uncles Eamon and Michael, who work full-time at the store, to play eighteen, an opportunity they do not pass up. It is the course, not the chance to spend another four hours with my grandfather, that draws them. They grew up playing here, but now that they have reached adulthood, none of them can afford the membership dues.

My grandfather's invitation to his sons is not motivated by nostalgia. He has something he needs to tell my father, but it has never been easy for him to talk to his middle son. Theobald—Teddy, at my grandmother's insistence—has always been a sourpuss, a worrywart, the only boy in the neighborhood who had to wear a mouth guard to bed to keep him from grinding his teeth to dust. Skittish and nervous—those were words that fit my father in his youth, and if my grandfather ever asked himself how he got that way, he probably laid it at the feet of my grandmother. *She must have babied him; the other boys never needed nicknames.* My grandfather hasn't noticed that years spent listening for sounds that never came—a calling from God, a jagged rainstorm of Russian missiles—have calmed my father, although the time away from home has done little to brighten his personality.

BY THE TIME the starter sends my father, uncles, and grandfather to the first tee, the sun is hammering at their backs. The air is gauzy and damp. The rain the night before should have softened the course, but the fairways are as stiff and brittle as the head of a broom. Pouring out of the trees that line the first fairway, the sheet-metal rattle of the cicadas grows louder and shriller as the temperature hikes into the nineties.

"Ah, Jaysus!" my grandfather says, slipping into the exaggerated brogue he uses when he is angry, or immoderately happy, or delivering the final line of a story. "Are we golfing or swimming?" He is plucking at his shirt, which sticks to his back and dampens wherever his fingers make contact with the fabric. He hates the sun for glaring at his defenseless Celtic skin. He hates sweating through his shirt before he reaches the turn at the ninth hole. He is not a prim man—no man his size could be called prim—but he is fastidious: his golf shirts are pressed, his irons glint in the sun, and at the end of the round he will take a toothbrush to the underside of his golf spikes.

"Too hot for you, Dad?" Eamon says. He cranes his head and stage-whispers to my father and Michael: "He's already looking for excuses for shooting a hundred."

My grandfather jerks his driver out of his golf bag and eyes his oldest son. "That's awfully big talk for someone who can't break par at New Paltz."

"Break par?" Eamon opens his arms wide, as if staggered by my grandfather's words. New Paltz is a public course, a short-yardage span of scorched grass and sandy tee boxes. "I shot an eagle last week."

"Likely a bald eagle," my grandfather says. "If your brothers were still in the army, they'd have to arrest you."

Before Eamon can respond, my grandfather cuts him off. "Now, quiet down. I didn't bring you here so you could run your mouth all day." But that is exactly why he brought Eamon and Michael to the golf course. My grandfather needs to work himself into a talking frame of mind and for that he needs an audience. A natural showman, he doesn't like one-on-one encounters. He prefers the stage of the hardware store, the barroom, or the golf course—places where men gather to trade stories rather than confidences.

At the store, a circle of older men gathers every Saturday morning to spend a few dollars and thirty minutes on the week's news. While my uncles fold their arms and laugh with the other men, my father tends the paint mixers at the back of the store. He hears the bursts of staccato laughter from the front, but the words are drowned out by the thudding of the cans blending pure pigments into flat colors.

FROM THE FIRST tee it is clear that it will be a long day for my father. His swing is rusty and his short game is a shambles. Each time one of my father's tee shots slices into the dense woods or a chip shot lands squarely in the open palm of a sand trap, my grandfather, usually not a sympathetic player, dispenses pats on the back and kind words—*Hang in there, Teddy, you'll get it together.* My grandfather is keeping his instincts in check; his first impulse is to ride my father about the way he's playing, to establish a laughing, back-and-forth patter with this young man the way he does with other men. The problem is that my father will not meet him halfway, or any way at all. With each hole he grows more frustrated by his inability to put the ball within fifty yards of where he wants it to go, and when he gets frustrated, my quiet and occasionally sullen father becomes quieter and more sullen. My grandfather is looking for the lever that will open his son's rigid jaw; what he has to say will be easier, he believes, if his son isn't giving him that sad-sack stare all day. He has made up his mind that a soft touch might be just the thing to put his son at ease, but my father will not respond and the effort is chafing at my grandfather. He keeps at it like a man camped in front of the nickel slots, expecting the next pull to be the one that lines up the cherries and disgorges the jackpot. He has already invested a pocketful of his patience, and he is beginning to consider other games where his bluff confidence can bully the table into submission.

My father is the last to tee off on the eighth, where the fairway pushes through a stand of pines before veering sharply toward the green. The safe play is to lay up on the turn and hope to reach the green with a long second shot. My father blasts his drive high and to the right, trying to shoot over the trees, cut the angle on the dogleg, and leave himself a short chip to the green. Eamon and Michael are laughing before he finishes his backswing.

"I think you spent too much time with the Eskimos," Eamon says. "Maybe in the North Pole, left is that way, but back here it's still this-a-way." He hooks his arm to the left to indicate the direction of the fairway, which my father has completely misplayed.

"I hear in Alaska they use dogsleds instead of caddies," Michael says. "So it must be throwing off your concentration not to have a bunch of dogs licking their balls between shots, right, Teddy?"

"Forget the sled dogs," Eamon says. "He's going to need a bloodhound to find that ball."

"Kiss my ass," my father says.

"Come on, Teddy," Michael says, "do you really think that's going to help your swing?"

"All right, that's enough out of the both of you." My grandfather has his hands raised, palms out, like a referee in a boxing match. "We don't need the crude talk, and I won't have you mocking your brother for the time he spent defending this country from the communists."

"Communists?" Eamon says. "Dad, he was in Alaska."

"And did the Russians invade while he was up there?"

"Well—"

"Well nothing. I say he must have been doing a mighty good job of it."

"We're just having some fun," Eamon says, "aren't we, Teddy?"

Before my father can open his mouth, my grandfather finishes the conversation. "It's not the kind of fun I want to be hearing today." Without looking at my father, he grabs his bag and stalks down the fairway. Michael and Eamon exchange a look—eyes rolling, a quick snort—and follow. My father is left to collect his bag and consider what has happened. He looks out at the retreating figure of my grandfather and sees a man who still thinks of his second son in the most damning terms for a family of boys: *moody, delicate, sensitive.*

"So what's next?" Michael says. He and my father are deep in the rough on the ninth, far from my grandfather and Eamon. They scan the thatch for their wayward Top-Flites, tasseled grass brushing their knees. "You figured out the next stop on the Teddy Dunn world tour?"

"Since when does Anchorage qualify as the world?" my father says.

"It's more than most people around here have seen," Michael says.

"Not more than you," my father says. "And you're still here."

"I've seen enough of the world." Michael locates his ball and kicks it from the tall grass to the edge of the fairway. "This place suits me just fine."

This is the closest that my father and my uncle will come to talking about Vietnam for the next twenty years. Michael is twenty-two and only one year removed from his hitch as a gunner in an air cavalry unit. Although he has always been the one who holds nothing sacred, the kid who made the other altar boys crack up in the middle of a funeral Mass, he doesn't talk about the war. Michael and my father had been close as boys—Eamon existed in his own world, breathing the rarefied air of the first-born son and the natural athlete—but sharing a bedroom was one thing, and finding words for the rough edges of experience was another matter entirely.

"So what about you?" Michael says. "I never thought you were all that crazy about living here."

"I don't know," my father says. "I was thinking of giving this place another chance." Until he says it, he hasn't been thinking of giving the town another try—not for any longer than it takes him to make a little money and figure out his next step. Army buddies have offered to help him find jobs in Texas, Arizona, Illinois, practically anywhere that isn't Wiltwyck.

But as quickly as the words are out of his mouth, they are embraced with the force of revelation by my father. For a month he has seen the way that Michael and Eamon talk to my grandfather—not about their lives and what they want out of them (who does *that?*), but about little things, such as when to have a sale on lawn mowers and what that jackass Rinaldi the grocer is up to—and suddenly he recognizes a yawning gap that his brothers have crossed without him. When my father left Wiltwyck for college, Eamon was at war with the old man over late nights and booze on his breath, and Michael was practically a kid, a joker who earned smiles of mock disapproval from his mother and his teachers and who willingly courted my grand-father's anger to earn himself a moment's attention. Now they talk like adults, if not exactly like equals, and my father cannot shake the feeling that he is still seen as the prickly teenager who flinched whenever my grandfather spoke. The remedy for this, which my father accepts quickly and completely, is to remain in town and in the store, where my grandfather will, eventually, recognize the change that has come over his second-born.

My father may even believe that this moment of recognition by my grandfather is already under way. Maybe *that's* what was going on at the eighth tee: The old man was trying to send a message that he was in Teddy's corner. He understood that after almost three years in the military, his middle son had started to come into his own, and he couldn't keep quiet when Eamon, the only son who hadn't served his country, tried to take him down a peg.

My father is still thinking this through when he tops his drive on the tenth. In the short seconds of silence that follow, the seal on my grandfather's frustration cracks. He is putting himself out there for a kid who can't even hit a goddamn golf ball. "I swear to God, Theobald," he says. "If you lose one more ball, it's com-ing out of your paycheck."

The sun is beating down on him, and his sweat-soaked shirt clings to his back. The things he needs to tell my father swell within him, but once he has started needling my father about the way he is playing, he cannot stop. He is the same way with alcohol and cigarettes: he can delay that first taste, but once the glass is filled or the match is struck, he hears the starter's pistol and the race is on.

"Are you sure you're not left-handed?" he says as my father digs in his pocket for another ball, then stoops to tee up. "Maybe you'd have more luck if you turned the club backward."

Eamon, two years older than my father, married and the father of twins, senses that it is open season on his brother. In high school, he was a three-sport star pursued by willing girls and eager college recruiters. But during the winter of his senior year, he rolled his car and cracked two vertebrae—an injury that kept him out of sports, out of college, and out of Vietnam. More than either of his brothers, he has modeled himself after the old man; to this day, he drinks only my grandfather's chosen brand of whiskey and smokes the same cigarettes. He is most comfortable at the head of the table or with his glass raised to deliver a toast, all eyes turned to him. Eamon also has my grandfather's way around an unkind observation. When my father shanks another drive on the sixteenth tee, he doesn't miss his chance: "I'd suggest you hit from the ladies' tees, Teddy, but that's not going to straighten out your slice."

THE GROUP APPROACHES the seventeenth green, where, two years earlier, my grandfather was shot while standing over a putt. A teenager named Richie Landgraf fired his father's deer rifle at a can of Genesee he had set on top of a fence post. He missed the can but hit my grandfather squarely in the backside. My grandfather couldn't sit comfortably for a month, but otherwise he emerged from the incident—"the assassination attempt," he called it—unscathed. He was back at work the following weekend, and the store was packed with well-wishers eager to hear the story from the man himself.

Although he was in Vietnam when it happened, Michael is always the one who tells the shooting story at Dunn family gatherings. Much of his version is an impression of the way my grandfather told it: Richie Landgraf's pose as he fired the gun, the look on my grandfather's face when the bullet fragments pierced his madras pants, the slow-motion topple to the manicured grass. The capper is Michael's way of doing my grandfather's brogue: "Like a hot poker it was, right up me arse."

Like all of the stories my family tells, this one is subject to a strict code: It does not belong to the person who lived it but to whoever tells it best. What does it matter if it was Teddy who backed the silver Eldorado into the side of the house? If Eamon tells it better—mimicking my grandfather's sputtering fury, my father's goggle-eyed stare, and the sound of the side-view mirror snapping off against the clapboard—then it becomes his to tell during a lifetime of Thanksgiving dinners. The same rule applies to all of our family lore, especially those stories that conjure my grandfather's spirit like a genie rising out of a bottle: the old man cruises the streets, high beams on, looking for Eamon in the early-morning hours after the junior prom; he drags his frostbitten sons deep into the wilds of the Catskills because men, he tells them, cut down their own Christmas tree; he emcees the annual talent show for the Knights of Columbus, his act getting bluer as the hour grows late and the glasses of Powers whiskey pile up.

We tell ourselves that these stories are important because they connect us to our shared history and prevent the dearly departed from ever really leaving us. But the endless catalog also keeps at bay the need to talk to each other. We are great at talking *about,* but we have never mastered talking *to.*

Standing on the apron of the seventeenth green, Michael calls out to his brothers: "Gentlemen! Gentlemen!" He removes his cap and bows his head. "A moment of silence, please, in honor of our father's celebrated buttock."

Eamon falls in line next to Michael, his head down, his hands folded in prayer, barely able to stifle a laugh. My father stands midway between his brothers and his father, and it takes him a moment to put the pieces together—time enough to feel like an outsider among the people who should be closest to him.

"Oh, for Christ's sake," my grandfather says. "No manners in this bunch."

"Honestly, Dad," Eamon says. "I can't believe they haven't put up a plaque yet."

"For posterior—I mean, posterity," Michael adds.

When did they learn to do this? my father wonders. How did they figure out how far they can push? And what does Dad see in them that makes this possible? The questions and his lack of answers make him acutely aware of what he has missed during the years spent away from the family: the seemingly insignificant moments, the accretion of inside jokes, and the common points of reference that are the closest most people ever come to intimacy. On the green, listening to the volley of comments from his father and his brothers, he feels the weight of every time he's had to ask Eamon or Michael to bring him up to speed on some story or some minor local scandal that has transpired in the past five years and to which someone in the store or at home or at church has made a passing, heavily freighted allusion.

"That's enough," my grandfather says as the blood rises in his ears like mercury. "A man likes to concentrate when he's showing his sons who's boss."

Even my father recognizes that they are pushing their luck and that one more word will ignite my grandfather's temper. They fall silent, holding their breath, barely shifting their feet on the buzz-cut grass. My grandfather leans over his putter, the rise and fall of the green as familiar to him as the layout of the hardware store. He taps the ball and it disappears into the hole. "Put me down for a three," he says, "and give the lot of you—what? Sixes?" He mutters something about manners and respect and the rules of the game. "That kind of foolishness," he says, "is why I don't ask you to play here."

Eamon and Michael wait until my grandfather storms off the green before they start laughing, and for the first time on the course my father smiles, and he and Eamon and Michael are three kids having a laugh at their father's expense, eager to finish their round and beg dimes from their mother for ice cream sandwiches at the snack bar.

ON THE EIGHTEENTH tee they are hot and tired and ready to finish their round. The store opened at six in the morning and the four of them have been together for close to twelve hours—far beyond any reasonable limit for family togetherness. My grandfather's shirt is glued to his back and all he wants is the air-conditioned refuge of the men's grill. *Maybe it can wait until Monday.* But then he thinks about my father shambling into the store at seven, that black cloud hanging over him, and he knows it has to happen today, before they reach the clubhouse.

"Teddy, I've been thinking about the store," he says. My father and grandfather are right of the green, my father in the sand trap, my grandfather on the stiff grass. Michael and Eamon are waiting on the green, out of sight and out of earshot.

My father is eyeing the flagstick, barely visible over the lip of the bunker. He is practicing his swing before stepping onto the sand, taking metronome-quick chops with his sand wedge. He turns and squints into the sun, which rides above my grandfather's head. "Aren't you always thinking about the store?" he says, and the smile returns, sly this time, gently prodding my grandfather. *So this is how it's done,* he thinks. *This isn't so hard.*

My grandfather appears to ignore him. He is moving the face of his pitching wedge into and out of the shadow he casts in front of himself. "What I've been thinking is, working there probably isn't the best thing for you."

Like smoke rising from a pile of burning leaves, that's how my father would remember my grandfather's tousle of white hair rising from his sunburned face. "You don't want me at the store?"

"I've just been thinking there are probably other things you'd rather do."

"What other things?" His voice is strained. There is no breath behind it.

"I don't know, Teddy," my grandfather says, perhaps more sharply than he intends. *That sun, this day; it's too much.* "You can do whatever you want."

"You don't want me at the store." It's a statement, although my father's voice falters at the end and it sounds like a question, or a plea.

"Listen, Teddy, there are plenty of other things you could do, and I think you should." He ends it there, with *should*. He nods, a quick, curt bob of the head that my grandfather uses to signal the end of a conversation. *All right, then,* it seems to say. *Enough of that.* "Now, are you going to take your shot?" He points the head of his wedge at my father's ball.

"Dad." My father swallows hard. He is not thinking about the ball sitting in the sand trap. He is focused on the lump lodged in his throat and the sharp pain it creates just below his Adam's apple. "What am I supposed to do?"

"Jesus Christ, just hit the ball," he says quietly, almost to himself.

My father says *Dad* again and it isn't a plea or a question or even a name. It is just a word and it hangs there between them, neither man able to make that short, fat syllable mean what he wants it to mean. My father wants it to be a splash of cold water that brings my grandfather to his senses and makes him realize that here, standing in front of him, is his son who has been out in the wilderness and is ready to come home. My grandfather hears it, hears the way it is said, and thinks of my father as a toddler on some distant August afternoon, covered in chocolate ice cream, desperate to be picked up and held. He remembers the way he shrank from the smeared face and sticky fingers, diverting the boy's chubby, clinging hands into my grandmother's lap.

My father wants to kick himself for so badly misreading his father's kindness on the front nine. The old man was setting him up; he wanted to find something kind to say to sweeten the pill, but all he could come up with was a joke about his son keeping the Russian hordes at bay. He could already hear his father telling that one at the front of the store, and all the men laughing.

My father tries to lock his eyes on my grandfather, but what he sees is the face of the fat orange sun. My grandfather looks down and threshes the dry turf with his club, willing the moment to pass, silently begging my father to turn around, take his shot, and relieve the pressure that has built like a vise around his heart.

MY FATHER HAS never told this story—never this way, never this much, never all at once.

When my father alludes to the events of that day, it isn't so much a story as it is a parable, compact and instructive, compressed into the hard certainty of a pearl—and like a pearl, it cannot be easily pried loose. In my father's version, there are no unanswered questions, no jagged unknowns. One day everything was fine—my father was stocking shelves and preparing for the switch from lawn mowers to snowblowers. The next day my grandfather told him that he could do whatever he wanted, as long as it wasn't in the store—not in so many words, but the message came through loud and clear. When my grandfather gave him a week to get his bags packed and hit the road (again, not in so many words), my father did him one better and left in two days.

As my father sees it, the events of that day illustrate two points. One, my grandfather was a hard man, comfortable in a crowd but closed like a fist with his wife and children. And two, my grandfather was a poor judge of character, because in the years that followed, my father took a job outside Boston, started telling people to call him Theo, met and married my mother, and built his own residential construction company. The day that the *Boston Globe* ran an article about my father's success in renovating historic homes, he held up the front page for all of us to see. "Not bad for a guy who wasn't good enough to work in a hardware store," he said.

My uncles were left to draw their own conclusions about his abrupt departure in the days after their round of golf. Teddy moved on to something else, like Teddy always did, and when my grandfather's death put the store in their hands, they were too busy to ponder why Teddy did the things he did. "Your father was always the lone wolf," Uncle Eamon once told me, and maybe it had been true for my father's whole life, or maybe it just became true for having been repeated so often in the decades that followed that day.

Over the years I have detected in my father the slow drift of certain facts. My uncles, once cast as villains for being chosen to continue my grandfather's legacy, were later seen as victims forced to keep the business on its feet as a tribute to their father's memory, despite the fading of Wiltwyck's downtown and the unwelcome appearance of a Home Depot just outside of New-burgh. But to my father, these minor shadings do not alter the fundamental truths of that day.

I am not so sturdy in my faith.

Perhaps my grandfather saw in my father's brief stints in college, the seminary, and the army evidence that his middle son was in pursuit of something he would never find in the hardware store's stockroom—and that looking for it there would only make him bitter long before his time. Maybe a month of watching my father at the paint mixers, straining to hear, or to blot out, the laughter of the men at the front of the store was all the proof he needed. Or maybe it was as simple as this: My grandfather knew that the store could never support himself, his sons, and their families, but admitting this—particularly to one of the sons embraced by the enameled Dunn & Sons sign—was more than his pride could take. So without the words to explain any of the financial and emotional calculus brewing in his head, he turned to my father and tried to send him into the world with a vote of confidence: *You can do whatever you want.*

If my grandfather had known that he had only four months left in him, or if he had lived to be eighty, he might have been able to explain himself to my father, and my father might have seen his departure from his hometown as something other than an exile. But expecting the old man to open his heart to one of his sons would be making him into someone he never could have been. Even in a family comfortable with the elastic properties of the truth, that kind of invention goes beyond embellishment and into the realm of make-believe.

Lately, the time I spend with my father is weighted with silences. During holiday visits, we drive to see how a cedar-shingled roof has weathered its first ice storm; we watch football games played between colleges we don't care about; we sit amid the crumpled wrapping paper late on Christmas morning staring intently into our coffee cups when we find that we are the only ones in the room. I know there is a razor-straight line that can connect the mute longing of my grandfather's fragile heart to my father's and even to mine, but whenever I start asking him the what-ifs and couldn't-it-bes, I am stymied by his you-don't-knows and you-weren't-theres. He folds his arms and sets his jaw and says these things as if they matter—as if he owns this story and the right to tell it. But it's always Michael who tells the shooting story. Only Eamon can mimic the sound of the El-dorado's mirror scraping the side of the house. For all the bitter drama of my father's memories of that day, there is so much that he doesn't know or has failed to imagine. He doesn't see what I can see: that the story just might save us if it is ever told the right way.

Look at Everything

The fire was an accident. Dugan was taking pictures and the grass against the side of the church was dry and brittle as hay. It was a small church, white clapboard with a peaked roof, and it sat at the end of a long gravel drive flanked by cottonwood trees and fields of red dirt. As he leaned against the wall to get a shot up the length of the steeple, he tossed his cigarette into the grass and walked to the other side of the church without once looking down. His eyes were fixed on the cross, stark against the sky, and he didn't know that the grass had caught until he saw the smoke wrapping its fingers around the church. The fire spread and spread until the whitewashed boards glowed orange, and the wind kept blowing until the wall was a curtain of flame. It happened so fast that Dugan was powerless to stop it. He winced at the heat on his face and scrambled into his car. The keys were already in the ignition, but somehow he couldn't take his eyes off the church, which glowed as if outlined in neon. The smoke reached into the sky, twisting into curlicues in the wind.

Dugan pounded his fists on the steering wheel as a bitter rush of *goddamn its* poured out of him—but he did not start the car and put the church behind him. Instead, he grabbed the camera, wrenched open the door, and began shooting. He darted around the church coughing and sweating, the sound of the fire like branches snapping in a storm. The wind billowed the cottonwoods at the edge of the field and pushed the fire onto the roof, and Dugan knew there was no stopping it. Only when he had filled the roll with the smoke and flames did he run back to the car and gun the engine, spinning a riot of gravel in the wheel wells.

Once he was out on the county road, his eyes raked the rearview mirror for signs of other cars, for anyone who might have seen him speeding away from the church. He thought for the first time about calling the police or the fire department and reached for the cell phone in the cup holder but withdrew his hand quickly, as if the phone were an ember flung by the fire. Even if they believed it was an accident, they were sure to ask why he'd spent so much time snapping pictures when he should have been calling for help.

He checked the rearview again, expecting a burst of police lights, an onrushing cruiser. Still nothing. Three miles from the church, he started to let himself believe he was in the clear. As his heart let loose a rush of blood, he wished there were someone in the passenger's seat, someone who had seen everything, from the moment he'd dropped the cigarette until now. Someone who could say, *It's not your fault. It just happened.* But the seat held only the camera, staring mutely back at him.

AT HOME, HE stripped in the middle of the kitchen and stuffed his clothes into the washing machine. He took a long shower, hoping the scalding water would purge him of the smoke and sweat and his own stupidity. He told himself that no one had been hurt, that it was just a building. A property crime. It was bad, but it could have been worse. But that night, as the local news led with a report about the church, it became clear to him just how bad it was. The pastor talked about the loss to the community, the shock that the mostly older, rural congregation felt. Some of the faithful might not find out about the fire until they showed up for services on Sunday, he said, and saw only a pile of charred boards. "I don't know who would do this," he said. "But I can only hope that God's love reaches into their heart and brings them back to the fold." An investigator from the Durham Fire Department said that the blaze was being treated as suspicious but that it was too soon to say if it was connected to the rash of fires at African-American churches in the Southeast earlier that spring.

Already it seemed too late for Dugan to come forward and explain what had happened. His only defense, that he was merely an idiot, wouldn't be believed. He hadn't even known that it was a black church. But people would see him only as a criminal and a racist. And what could he ever say to Claire? That it was all just an accident? She had already left for New York without him—the summer would give them both a chance to reevaluate, she'd said—but if she ever found out that he'd just burned down a church, that he'd run from the scene, that he had no plans to turn himself in... that would be the end of them.

HE BARELY SLEPT that night, expecting a knock on the door, red and blue lights pulsing all along the street. The next morning, the newspapers in Durham and Raleigh each ran a picture on the front page of the blackened remains of the church. People were angry and frightened. They talked about the fire as a step backward, as a sign that the old ways were making a comeback.

Driving to work in the morning, Dugan was convinced that everyone would be able to smell the smoke on his skin. He managed an art-house movie theater in Chapel Hill and usually spent most of his shift in the back office or the projection booth. But that day, he worked the concessions counter, hoping the smell of hot oil and melted butter would mask the evidence of the fire. When his shift ended, he raced home to shower and then drove to the community college for his twice-a-week photography class, never once breaking the speed limit. He'd thought about going straight home after work—holing up and watching the news to find out if the police had any leads on the fire—but he figured the best thing to do was to stick to his routine. Sudden changes might arouse suspicion. Here he was, already thinking like a criminal. A fugitive from justice.

The class was taught by a woman named Lillian who sported the short haircut and spiky bangs favored by artsy women over sixty—a style Claire called a Premarin Pixie. Lillian wore chunky necklaces and bracelets that, to Dugan's eye, could have been made of plastic or bone or Chiclets. She encouraged her students to find the beauty in everyday objects: paper clips, hubcaps, shopping carts, laundry hanging on a line. "Beauty isn't something you make," she told the class. "It's something you find."

For the summer session, Lillian had assigned each of the students a location to explore for their portfolios. She'd chosen the subjects at random, to encourage her students to embrace serendipity. Dugan's slip of paper had read CHURCHES. He couldn't even guess how many roadside chapels he passed driving from his house to the theater to the college: Lighthouse Missionary Baptist Church, Salt of the Earth Church of God in Christ, Rock of Ages Holiness Church . . . the list went on. It had been during his day off from work yesterday that he stumbled across the little white church with the peaked roof and the tall steeple and turned off the county road to take a closer look.

There were ten people in the class. Hippie Chick was in her twenties and talked a lot about beauty, which meant anything natural, and ugliness, which was anything made of metal, plastic, or concrete. Trees were beautiful; so was the ocean. Cars and telephone poles were ugly. Five people said they were taking the class because they wanted to be pet photographers, which Dugan had never realized was such a booming industry. There was Christian Dad, who wanted to take pictures of his daughter that would be "suitable for framing" and who said

"Merry Christmas!" instead of cursing whenever he made a mistake in the darkroom. There was also Punk Rock Girl and Real Estate Lady, who carried a briefcase and wore frothy pastel suits. Sometimes he wondered what they called him: Beard Guy. Weird Guy. Weird Beard Guy.

That night, as the class started, Lillian turned on the projector and showed slides of atomic-bomb tests conducted in the Pacific Ocean in the 1950s. With each mushroom cloud, she recited the location of the test as if it were the Latin name of a tropical plant: Bikini Atoll. Enewetak. Mururoa. Kiritimati. When she finished she switched on the lights and faced her blinking students. "Well?" she said. "Thoughts?"

"Disgusting," Hippie Chick said. Her tangled blond hair was held back by yarn, and she wore a loose-fitting dress and sandals. "It's like looking at the face of the devil."

The others in the room cast their eyes down at the table or up at the blank screen. They didn't care about the slides. Most of them wanted to commiserate about how difficult it was to get a dog to sit still once you put a hat on it.

"Anybody else?" It was obvious what Lillian wanted—she wanted them to find the beauty. "Focus on the picture," Lillian said. "Just the image, on its own terms."

Still no one else spoke. There were nights when Dugan gave her the answer she was looking for, not because he agreed with her or because he wanted to move on to the finer points of pet photography, but because he couldn't bear the sight of Lillian floating up there, ignored by a roomful of people. That alone might have been reason enough to say something. Except, tonight, he did see the beauty. In black-and-white the clouds looked like mushrooms, but in color, they weren't mushrooms at all. They were pulsing flowers of orange, yellow, and red, blooming a million fiery petals into the blue sky. The images seemed to ooze upward. If it were possible to sculpt with lava, this is what it would look like.

"It's kind of beautiful, right?" Dugan said. "I know there's an island being vaporized, but as long as there's nobody on the island, what's the harm?" Around the room eyebrows raised and a few heads shook. Comments like that, he realized, were why no one ever talked to him during the break.

"The harm?" Hippie Chick said. "What about the environment?"

"There are other islands," Dugan said. "It's not like they blew up the only one, is it?" He looked around the room, a gallery of averted gazes.

"It's pure destruction," Hippie Chick said. "It's evil."

"I didn't say it was good or evil. I just said it was sort of beautiful." As the words left his mouth, he got the lurching sense that he had said too much—that he had let himself get swept away in Lillian's nonsense.

Lillian inhaled sharply, a cue that she was about to resume speaking, when a voice piped up from the back of the room.

"I agree with him, sorta," Punk Rock Girl said. "I don't think it matters if it's beautiful or ugly. You've got to look at everything." Lillian nodded and scanned the room, her eyes wide in an effort to reignite the discussion. Dugan slouched lower in his chair and Hippie Chick made an audible *tsk*.

"Okay," Lillian said, "let's pick up the discussion we were having in the last class about the pros and cons of tripods."

AFTER AN HOUR and a half, the class had a ten-minute break. As they all filed into the courtyard that separated the school from the parking lot, Dugan steered himself away from the others and pulled a cigarette from the pack.

"You shouldn't smoke," Punk Rock Girl said.

She was narrow-shouldered and young, barely out of high school. She had a ring in her nostril, two more in one eyebrow, and too many to count in her ears. Her hair, glossy black and streaked with pulpy red, was cut in a severe bob. With her dark eyes and loops of silver wire, she looked like Theda Bara on acid. She smiled, a row of perfect teeth. She'd had braces. Expensive ones.

"You shouldn't tell people what to do," Dugan said.

"You want to get cancer?" She said it lightly, like a joke, and again flashed those unstained teeth. Her final portfolio, he recalled, was going to be a series of pictures taken at a chicken-processing plant.

"There are worse things," he said, exhaling a plume of smoke. "Besides, it keeps the tobacco farmers in business."

"So smoking is your way of supporting capitalism?" she said, the smile disappearing.

"You don't sound like you're from around here," Dugan said. Her voice was flat, accentless. A voice from a sitcom, auto-tuned by ennui.

"I'm supposed to be in Oakland," she said.

"Well, that explains it."

"My mother is what explains it."

Okay, Dugan thought, *not barely out of high school—still there.* Likely one of the faculty brats who haunted the coffee shops in their thrift-store jackets and clunky shoes.

"What about you?" she said. "You don't sound like you're from down here."

"Chicago," he said, taking another long drag.

"And why would you ever leave there for here?"

His gaze drifted above the long, low-slung buildings of the community college. "I guess you could say I did it for love."

She smirked, but to Dugan it was true—though it left a lot out. He checked his watch and dropped the cigarette, careful to crush it under his foot before going inside.

DUGAN AND CLAIRE had met as first-years at the University of Chicago and almost from the beginning, they'd been inseparable. Movies at Doc Films were followed by heated discussions over garlicky slices of pizza at the Medici. All-nighters in the library led straight to greasy breakfasts at Salonica. He was going to be a film critic and a director, like his hero Jean-Luc Godard; Claire was going to be a graphic novelist with a small but intense cult following. After graduation, they were the first among their friends to get married. Dugan started working at an independent movie theater on the North Side—it was like getting paid to go to film school, he said. Claire waited tables and devoted time to a webcomic about philosophically inclined penguins; in each installment, one of the penguins was eaten by a polar bear. They saw bands at pop-up festivals and plays at store-front theaters. They shopped in vintage stores and swam in Lake Michigan. But they were always broke, and as they got closer to thirty, what a nineteenth-century novel would have called *their prospects* seemed to be drying up. Claire's webcomic got fewer and fewer visits, and for all the movies that Dugan saw, he wasn't making any progress on a screenplay or attracting much interest with his occasional movie reviews. Every month they fell farther behind, unable to keep up with bills from credit cards, student loans, and collections agencies—all the borrowed money of their entry to adulthood.

Late one night in bed, in the small, shabby apartment that Craigslist had described as a *cozy Victorian,* Dugan had said, "One of us has to go to law school." They were no good with numbers and bad at science, so finance and medicine were out. Law school seemed like the only way to avoid a future of similar apartments and service-economy jobs. Both lay still, breathing in the darkness and listening to the skittering of mice in the walls, the knocking of the radiators that never produced any heat. Claire broke the silence: "I'll do it."

Dugan always said that if Claire had waited two seconds longer, then he'd be the one in law school. It was that close.

In the year that followed, Claire landed a spot at Duke Law. Along with her near-perfect LSAT scores—Claire had always been a whiz at standardized tests—she had submitted an archive of her comic, in which the penguins wrestled with questions of fate and free will in the face of an uncaring po-lar bear. Dugan knew they were in for a change when they packed for the move, but back then—it seemed like someone else's life now—they figured it would be only three years and then they'd be back in Chicago. Claire would be at a law firm in the Loop, and as for Dugan? Well, he had three years to figure that out.

He had anticipated that her classes would take up a lot of time, but he hadn't counted on just how much. And it wasn't just classes; it was the library, study groups, happy hours, and eventually moot court and law review. Every day during her first year, it seemed, he was on the phone saying, "Don't worry about it, I understand, I'll see you when you get in." Eventually he stopped answering his phone, let her calls go to voice mail, and signed up for a photography class. Stanley Kubrick had started out as a photographer, he told Claire, and there was plenty he could learn from the course about composition and light. Claire told him that she'd assumed the best way to become a filmmaker was to make a film, but Dugan assured her that he had a plan. What he didn't say was that he liked having somewhere to be that wasn't work or the empty house they'd rented. And that he was at his best when he was with her, but suddenly she was never around. He also found that he missed the rhythms of the school year: first day, projects, end of the semester, repeat. As he progressed through Lillian's classes, he had even started to imagine a future where Claire was a high-powered lawyer and he was a semi-famous photographer; a photojournalist, maybe, or an artist.

Everything seemed to be going according to plan until Claire's third year. She had an offer from a firm in New York City, and the fact that she was even considering it provoked a fight—the biggest they'd ever had. Dugan said Claire was reneging on their deal, selling out, becoming someone he didn't recognize. Claire, for her part, accused him of giving up, of coasting, of not being the same Dugan she had once known. The argument would flare and recede throughout the spring, and when Claire finally decided on New York, she told Dugan that she wanted them to take a break. To think of the summer as a trial separation, though Dugan knew that he was the one on trial. Claire would use the summer as evidence of his ability—or inability—to get his life in gear, to find his purpose, to make something happen. He'd put in almost three years at the movie theater, but that apparently didn't count. And neither did his photography, which Claire considered a hobby, nothing more.

He had seen this movie before. A character is forced to choose between a new, dream-come-true kind of life and the old life with its shabby house, broken dreams, and loving spouse. Only this wasn't a movie, and even before the fire, the chances were slim that Claire was going to stumble through the front door with her New York haircut and New York clothes and take Dugan in her arms and say, *Promise you'll never let me go!*

THE THURSDAY AFTER the fire, while the others cut mats for their prints, Lillian asked to see Dugan at the back of the room. She was wearing a button pinned to her dress—the word HATE with a diagonal red line through it.

"Dugan," she said. "I'm sure you know about the fire at the church."

Dugan blanched. "Such a terrible thing," he said, trying to sound vague, noncommittal.

"And you especially must feel the weight of it." Before Dugan could compose an answer—*Where was she going with this?*—Lillian placed a hand on his arm and continued. "While you're celebrating these sacred spaces, someone else is bent on destroying them. It makes the work you're doing all the more important."

Dugan nodded and *uh-huh*ed while Lillian spoke of the need to demonstrate to the congregation, to the state, even to the nation, that Durham was a city that would not tolerate this kind of hate crime. That's where Dugan came in. What she was hoping, Lillian said, squeezing his arm, and she knew this was a long shot, was that he might have taken some pictures of the church before this tragic act.

Dugan tried to speak but his voice caught in his throat. The roll he had taken at the church was at the house, buried in a bedroom drawer.

"I just think images like that could really help the community." Lillian dropped her voice and spoke to Dugan in a solemn tone. "You know, with the healing."

The healing. Lillian was offering a way for the pictures—some of the pictures, the ones taken *before* the fire—to serve a purpose. They could help with the healing, and that had to count for something. The callers on local talk radio were convinced that the arsonist would burn in hell, but Dugan was willing to grab for second chances wherever he could find them.

"I think I might have some pictures of that church," he said. "Not developed, but—"

"That would be so wonderful," Lillian said. There was going to be a special service on Sunday, and she wanted Dugan's photos on display. She had friends on the organizing committee who would be thrilled to see the pictures.

At the word *thrilled,* Dugan let a smile spread across his face. A committee thrilled to see his pictures. A whole community, healed. He doubted that it would help him with Claire, but there had to be *something* karmic about it, didn't there? He'd made an awful mistake, but now he was being given a way to reset the balance, if only a little.

Discreetly, Lillian handed him a key to the darkroom; she didn't want the other students to think he was getting special privileges.

The trip from the college to his house and back took almost an hour, and by the time he returned, the photography studio was deserted. Working quickly, he compiled the contact sheet, with its comic-book version of the fire. The first shot was the front of the church, its double doors and hand-lettered sign: TREE OF LIFE MISSIONARY BAPTIST CHURCH. The next few frames showed the church from the side, up the length of the steeple, with its clapboard in extreme close-up. On the drive over, he had admonished himself repeatedly not to print the pictures of the fire, even though he would be the only person in the building. But with one glimpse of smoke on the contact sheet, he felt his resistance begin to crumble. It was the fourteenth picture on the roll: the roofline bisecting the frame, wisps of smoke clearly visible on the right. In the images that followed, dense black smoke caught in the wind and spiraled around the narrow steeple. With the loupe pressed to his eye, he strained to see if smoke was visible in the earlier shots. He wanted to find the exact frame where it first appeared, the moment the camera noticed, even before he did, that something had gone awry. He wouldn't keep them, of course — that would be suicide — but maybe he could enlarge a few, just a few, and then destroy them after he'd had a really good look. He printed one, then another, and then another, clipping the pictures to the drying line as they emerged from their chemical bath.

He was swishing a print in one of the pans when the *click-whoosh* of the darkroom door sounded. He turned, a print flopping from the tongs in his right hand.

"Hey, Cancer Man, what are you doing here?"

Dugan flinched, and his eyes darted from Punk Rock Girl's face to the row of pictures suspended between them. "You're not supposed to be here." He was trying to sound authoritative, but he knew it had come out shaky.

"I've got my own key," she said, touching the edge of one of the prints, turning it so the image faced her. "I come here all the — ".

He saw in her eyes the moment that it hit her.

"Oh my God," she said, her face twisting into a knot. "You're the guy!" She took a step back, her hand half turning the knob of the inner door.

"It was an accident," he said, starting to yank the prints from the line.

She reached for the last picture he had developed, a bold slash of smoke pouring over the building. Dugan grabbed for it, creasing the paper and smearing his hands on the slick surface, but she snatched the print away from him.

"You've got to believe me," Dugan said. "I didn't know what was happening until it was too late. There was nothing I could do."

She narrowed her eyes at him and glanced down at the photo: blue sky, white wood, black smoke. Her face softened, but he couldn't tell if it was a smile or a smirk. "Whoa," she said. "This is amazing."

"I'm going to throw them all out," he said. "I promise."

"You're not going to use them for your portfolio?"

"Are you nuts?" Dugan sputtered.

"You burned down a whole church and you're not even going to keep the pictures?" Her voice echoed in the small room.

Dugan felt surrounded by noise and the girl and the evidence of what he'd done. His eyes jumped from her face to the picture she held to the prints still hanging on the line. "I want to forget it ever happened," he said.

"But you took all these pictures," she said.

Dugan stared hard at her, his face as hot as it had been outside the church. He had been wondering about that for three days, but he hadn't been able to figure out why he'd taken up his camera and started shooting instead of just driving away. As each print emerged from the pan, he had the growing sense that this was the best work he had ever done. That when faced with the flaming church, he had responded the way an artist would—but not, he had to admit, as a person should.

The girl was smiling again, casting her eyes to the drying line. "So how many are there?"

Dugan wanted to turn away from her, but he couldn't. "About half a roll."

"Half a roll," she said. "But it was an accident."

She looked straight at him, her pupils huge in the red glow of the darkroom. A minute ago, she had reached for the door, seemingly afraid of being alone with him. Now Dugan eyed the exit, weighing his chances for escape. She stepped closer.

"So," she said, "you want some help?"

Punk Rock Girl—whose real name was Chandra—told Dugan that she had been into photography since she was, "like, ten years old" and that she was only taking the class for access to the darkroom. Her mother's house wasn't far from the community college, in a neighborhood where a lot of other professors lived. "You think I could actually learn anything from old Lillian?" she said as she coaxed from the negatives a wave of flame barreling up the side of the church and fans of smoke sweeping over the steeple. "'Find the beauty!' Give me a break."

They printed every picture on the roll, the shots of the church before the fire for Lillian and a complete set of twenty-four for Dugan. He told Chandra he wanted to see the whole sequence, start to finish, just once, and then he was going to burn all the prints and the negatives.

She smiled and said, "Of course you will."

THE SUNDAY SERVICE was held at a local high school, and by the time Dugan arrived, the gymnasium was packed. It was just as

Lillian had predicted: Hundreds of people—black, white, and brown—had turned out in jackets and ties or in floral dresses and hats tied with extravagant bows. The stifling room buzzed with conversation and the flapping of photocopied programs pressed into service as fans. Dugan thought of shedding his blazer but could already feel his back soaked, his armpits damp. Without the jacket, he would look like a drowning man. He was picking his way through the folding chairs on the basketball court when Lillian spotted him and waved him toward the front. She was saving a seat for him, and for the first time Dugan saw that his pictures—the pre-fire pictures—lined the back wall of the gym. Lillian had scanned the prints and enlarged them to poster-size. She squeezed his arm and told him that everyone loved his work.

Dugan craned his neck, taking in the growing crowd. A few rows back he spotted the vivid red streaks in Chandra's hair, and before he could sit and pretend he hadn't seen her, she waved at him. He raised a hand weakly, more a tremor than a greeting. Chandra brought her hand to her mouth, turned an imaginary key between her lips.

The service lasted almost two hours. One after another, priests and ministers, a rabbi and an imam, took the podium to offer words of comfort to the congregation of Tree of Life and promises of support in their efforts to rebuild. Already, people from all over the state had donated money, building supplies, temporary meeting spaces, whatever the pastor and his flock needed. The pastor himself—the man Dugan had seen on television—spoke last, and he vowed to rebuild the church, larger than the old one and full to the rafters every Sunday.

The church was more than a building, the pastor said, more even than a house of God. The fire was a reminder that in this country, some people still thought they got to do the burning and others just got burned. But no more. The community was coming together, rising out of the ashes. There was a power greater than any man-made fire, and that was the righteous fire of the Holy Spirit. As the cries of "Amen!" echoed in the gym's vaulted ceiling, Dugan tried to feel that he was a part of this new community—hadn't he helped with the healing?—but the facts chewed at his insides. He could see himself only as some kind of saboteur. An impostor. A double agent.

After a closing prayer, the crowd migrated toward long tables where piles of doughnuts surrounded urns of coffee and pitchers of sweet tea. While Lillian rounded up some friends she wanted Dugan to meet, he scanned the room for an escape route, then knifed through the crush of bodies pressing in to see his pictures. He couldn't spend another minute shaking hands and being told what a blessing he had provided with his photographs. As for Chandra—what was she doing here? He could only imagine that the chance to see him sweating under the glare of all this goodwill was too tempting to pass up. Here was a girl who needed other hobbies.

As suddenly as his thoughts had turned to her, Chandra was at his side, as if he'd summoned her. She'd traded the tank top for a close-fitting chinoiserie dress—a black-and-red swirl of drag-ons chasing their tails. She was wearing fewer earrings and she'd pulled one of the loops out of her eyebrow. This apparently was her Sunday best.

Without a word, she dug her bitten-down nails into his wrist and steered him toward an exit under one of the basketball hoops. Dugan shook free of her. He glowered and asked why she was stalking him.

"In your dreams," she said. "My mom is on one of these committees for the people whose church was mysteriously burned down. She was so excited when I told her I wanted to come today—she thinks it's a sign of maturity."

"Your mother is in Lillian's group?"

"Are you kidding? Lillian's nobody. My mom teaches at the law school—she's kind of a big deal."

At the mention of the law school, the heat in the room flared. This was supposed to be a three-season blazer, but summer in the South wasn't one of those seasons. With a glance over his shoulder, he ducked through the door, Chandra close behind. A short hallway led to the parking lot.

"So you're, like, a big hero," Chandra said, once they were outside. "Without you, none of this—"

"Keep it quiet, will you?" Dugan spoke through gritted teeth. "Don't worry about it."

"I am going to worry about it. Have you told anyone?"

She made a dismissive pop with her tongue. "Who am I going to tell?"

"I don't know—your big-deal mother?"

"As if," she said.

"Friends at school?"

"Not a problem there."

"Your boyfriend?"

Chandra stuck out her tongue—pierced, Dugan saw, with a silver ball that sat like a pearl on the center. "Look, Dugan," she said. "I'll stop stalking if you stop flirting."

He was sure that he blushed. He felt the heat extend to his ears. He would never—

"Hey, where's your wife, anyway?" she said. "Or is that ring just, like, jewelry?"

"She's in New York," Dugan said.

"What's she doing there?"

"You'd have to ask her that," he said.

"Ouch," Chandra said. "So I guess the honeymoon is over."

"It's really none of your—"

"But you did tell her about your—what did you call it?— your accident?" Chandra pantomimed smoking, then casually dropping the butt over her shoulder. She made an O with her mouth in silent-movie shock.

"Could you please not mention it? Ever. To anyone."

She leaned in close, her voice a sharp whisper: "Do you really think you'd be here if I'd told anyone? You'd be, like, in prison or something."

He had begun to let himself believe that the odds of his being connected to the fire waned with every day that passed and that in another week or two the police would add the church's burning to the list of unsolved crimes and move on to something else. But all he had was this shaky assurance that Chandra hadn't said anything, yet.

"It's our little secret," she said. "But the next time you do it, you have to take me with you."

"There isn't going to be a next time."

"Oh, come on," she said. "You took *how many* pictures? There must have been *something* that you liked about it."

He wanted to deny it, but the truth was that when he was taking the pictures, he'd felt that electric sense he hadn't had in years—not since Chicago, when he and Claire had collaborated with some friends on a musical version of *The Gulag Archipelago*.

"Was it the heat?" Chandra said. "The color? Did you find the beauty?"

He and Claire had stayed up late for weeks, writing songs and dialogue, pushing furniture around their friends' apartment as they shuffled from scene to scene. Taking the pictures had brought it all back.

"It must be a rush to destroy something that big," Chandra said.

Dugan blinked as if he were trying to snap himself out of a trance or wake from a dream. "You just want to burn something down, don't you?"

She shrugged. "Why not? I mean, you did it."

Dugan didn't answer. There was no point in protesting his innocence, not to Chandra. All he had done was drop one cigarette, but the grass and the heat and the wind had turned it into something bigger than he could control.

"Come on," she said. "Nobody gets hurt, and some lucky congregation gets a better church out of it. You're practically Robin Hood."

"No," he said, but barely, and then he said it again, louder, trying to sound more assured. But Chandra was already walking away from him, back toward the gymnasium where the assembled crowd was making plans for the future against the backdrop of Dugan's photographs.

It still surprised him to find the house empty. He often came home and half expected to hear Claire making a cup of tea or tapping out an assignment on her laptop. The house was small—four rooms on a single story—but he still felt like he was rattling around inside it. In the kitchen, he opened a beer and peeled off his jacket and tie, then threw his shirt and pants in the washing machine. Though he pulled on a clean pair of jeans and a T-shirt, he couldn't shake the smell of wood smoke on his skin, in his hair, on his breath. Eventually his own body would give him away. He set the beer on the kitchen table, where he had spread out the photos, one after the other, looking again for the exact moment when the smoke was first visible. He had spent the weekend examining them, straining to see any sign of smoke before the pale ribbon that skirted the upper corner of photo 14. He could locate nothing. And yet photo 13, apparently an unblemished image, was taken at a moment when the fire was already burning. It just wasn't yet in his field of view.

He laid his phone on the table beside the photos and out of habit started playing Claire's old voice mails. When she left for New York, he'd begun compiling a record of her old voice mails and texts—almost three years' worth, with dates and times and handwritten notes about each call or message. He thought he'd managed to isolate the sequence that marked when things really started to go wrong, early in her third year of law school. It was sometime after this message:

Hey, sweetie. Study group is running late, so I'm going to grab dinner here and then head back to the library. Hope you're having a good day. Love you!

But it must have been before this one:

Dugan! Pick up! Why don't you ever answer? Look, it's late, I need to finish this brief. I'm going to crash at Kate's. See you to-morrow.

Dugan often wondered if there had been more to her interest in New York than just the job—and if the fight it provoked had been part of Claire's plan all along. He half believed that she'd met someone else—a classmate; a professor, even. That she'd been lying to him, and he hadn't caught on in time to put a stop to it. He almost wanted it to be true, that she was the disloyal one, that the dissolution of what they'd had was her fault. And if it was true, then her call for a trial separation was a sham, a way of letting Dugan down easy. He didn't have any evidence other than her late nights and the noticeable change in her feelings for him: he couldn't remember the last movie they'd seen together or the last pizza they'd shared. Dugan didn't have many other dots to connect, but he kept coming back to a glimpse of her suitcase lying open on the bed, well stocked with new underwear. He hadn't seen her in anything but the same cotton undies she'd worn for years, but she was leaving for the city with tightly rolled packs of bikinis and boy shorts whose crisp, lacy edges filled him with longing and despair. Thinking back on that moment, he had the sudden, weightless feeling of a cartoon character who looks down and realizes that he has already walked off the cliff. There was nothing to do but fall.

DUGAN SPENT MONDAY, his day off from the theater, at home. He didn't want to go out, didn't want anything new or different or unexpected to happen. He took another long shower, washed his sheets and towels, and decided to hold a private Kubrick film festival for himself: *Spartacus; 2001: A Space Odyssey; A Clockwork Orange*. On Tuesday morning, he grabbed the newspaper out of his neighbor's driveway and saw the headline: SECOND CHURCH BURNS. His stomach lurched, and he spent his day at the theater torn between competing thoughts. The second fire was good, because he didn't do it, and when they caught the person who did, they would probably pin the first fire on him too. And the second fire was bad, because he'd given the arsonist the idea and thus was the inspiration for another crime. In other words, the second fire was good for him legally but most likely bad for him karmically.

He was certain that Claire's penguins had puzzled over a similar issue in her webcomic; one of the penguins was a pragmatist, another a hardheaded idealist. But what was Dugan supposed to do? He and Claire hadn't so much as spoken in almost a month, and now he was going to see if she had any thoughts about the ethics of burning down a church?

At the start of Tuesday's class, Lillian used Dugan's photographs as an example of what she called "the timeless power of art." Last night's fire had only made the stakes clearer, she said. Dugan was on the front lines against the forces of bigotry, and for that, she said, he deserved a round of applause. The clapping was sporadic, arrhythmic, like coins tumbling out of a vending machine. Chandra, sitting in the back, clapped loudest and longest. It wasn't until the clapping subsided that Dugan noticed she had changed her hair. Oily black had been replaced with bright orange, tipped at the ends with yellow and blue. She told Lillian it was a show of solidarity with the churches that had been burned, and Lillian said it was lovely, just . . . lovely.

During the break, Dugan went outside to his usual spot near the concrete benches. Hippie Chick, Christian Dad, and one of the future pet photographers stood closer to the building, talking in low voices. If they didn't like him before, when he was just the guy in the back of the room admiring mushroom clouds, then they hated him after ten minutes of Lillian telling them how important his work was. Ten minutes that could have been spent talking about the proper shutter speed for shooting a dog catching a Frisbee.

Chandra bounded up to Dugan and asked for a cigarette.

"What about cancer?" he said.

"Worse things, right?" she said.

For a minute they smoked in silence, Chandra stifling a cough.

"I didn't have anything to do with it," Dugan said.

"With what?" Her eyes were dewy—if he didn't know her better, he'd say they were innocent—but her smile simmered. "Oh, the fire last night? Of course you didn't."

"I didn't," he said, louder than he'd intended.

"I know." Smoke jetted from her pursed lips. "I set it," she said, and a smile bloomed.

The cigarette fell from his fingers. If his life were a movie, the camera would have come in close, filling the frame with his stricken face.

"And I've got to tell you, you made it sound really easy, and it's not. It's hard as hell. It took me forever to get that place burning." Chandra's face was bright and untroubled.

He grasped for something to say. He thought of Dave in *2001,* trying to reason with HAL 9000. Chandra was launching all of his escape pods.

"Look, I did you a favor," Chandra said. "I made sure it was a white church. Now nobody thinks we're racists."

"Chandra, there's no 'we.'"

The lights in the parking lot had come on and moths were thwapping against the sodium bulbs. The other students were filing back into the building.

Dugan turned away from Chandra and began walking, eager to put distance between them. Then he stopped and looked at her. "You're just doing this to piss off your mother, aren't you?"

"No," she said petulantly. "This is great for my mother. She gets to be on TV, talking about what a tragedy this is and how much farther we have to go as a nation and blah-blah-blah."

"And you get to laugh at her because you know the real story."

Chandra picked at one of the buttons pinned to her camera strap—some band Dugan had never heard of. "Our secret, right?"

Dugan was exhausted. He glanced toward the building in the faint hope that the familiarity of the studio—its chemical smells and sharp corners, Hippie Chick's scowls, Lillian's certainty that beauty could be found in even the worst scenes—would keep his head from splitting into two raw and unbeautiful halves.

"Hey," Chandra said, extending one hand, "let's go for a ride."

A fire truck raced past the far end of the parking lot, sirens blaring, red and yellow lights punching holes in the darkness.

"Is that one of yours?" he said.

"Be nice," she said. She took two steps toward him and reached for his shoulder, but he brushed her hand aside.

The fire engine rounded a corner, and the shriek of its sirens Dopplered to a low whine. Dugan dug his hand into his pocket and squeezed his keys; the metal teeth bit into his hand. He felt the world spinning under him, faster than he could keep up. Let Chandra tell. Tell her mother, tell the police, tell Claire, tell everyone. Let it all come out. His head wobbled on his shoulders, a slow, silent *no* directed at all of the things he had put in motion and could not stop.

"I have to go," he said, and without looking back he let his shaky legs carry him into the parking lot.

WHEN HE ARRIVED home, the house was dark, the driveway empty. Why did he keep expecting it to be otherwise? Inside, on the table, lay the notebook devoted to Claire's voice mails and texts, along with the photographs of the church, still arranged in order, as if daring someone to connect the dots in the only direction they could lead. The notebook had been Claire's, and after he'd begun transcribing her messages, he found on a back page a sketch for one of Claire's penguin comics—a sketch she had made in law school. The polar bear had just eaten one of the penguins, and the two survivors sat alone on an ice floe. "Why do bad things happen to good penguins?" one of them said. In the next panel, the other penguin answered: "Who says he was a good penguin?"

You know the real story, he'd said to Chandra, and Dugan knew it too. The real story was that no matter how long the silence had lasted on that night in their Chicago bedroom, Claire was the only one who was ever going to say "I'll do it." Dugan knew it. And he understood that Claire had always known it too. That she was willing to do the work to save them, and do it without complaint, but Dugan wasn't. He'd been given three years to build a better future—one that they could share—and all he'd done was burn down a church. He wanted to believe that some things were just ready to burn and that the friction of the world turning, faster and faster every day, was all the spark that was needed.

But there was another part of the real story that only he knew. Before he'd taken the first picture of the fire, he'd stood in front of the church and just watched it burn. Not for long, but long enough. He felt the searing heat of the flames on his skin; heard the fire howl like the rush of a storm. He had come across a church and now it was becoming something else. It could never go back to what it was. *Look at what I've done,* he said to himself. *Look at what I've done.*

The Drive

The parents have been out. Now the parents come home tired, they come home smiling, they come home angry, they come home drunk.

THE MOMS ASK, How did it go? The moms ask, Did the kids give you any trouble? The moms say, Thanks for giving up your Saturday night. The moms ask, How is soccer? How is ballet? How was the play? The moms ask about college visits, about early decision. The moms get dirt on teachers, on other girls, on other kids, on other moms. Really? the moms say. That's too bad, the moms say. I had no idea.

THE DADS GO the bathroom. The dads piss loudly. The dads have taken off their coats and need to pull them back on. The dads forgot about the drive. The dads stand at the doors, waiting for the moms to stop talking. The dads do the math, shuffling through bills, fives and tens. The dads fold the money. Here you go, the dads say. Do we need to include hazard pay? The dads say, You've earned it.

THE MOMS LOOK like moms. Or the moms look like they don't want to admit that they're moms. Or the moms look the way the girls want to look one day when the girls are moms. The moms hope the girls are looking at them and thinking: option three.

THE GIRLS PACK up their homework: calculus, French, chemistry, English. The girls have big exams coming up. The girls have papers due on Monday. The girls are reading *Hamlet*. The girls are reading *Persepolis*. The girls are reading *Antigone, The Scarlet Letter, Jane Eyre, Pride and Prejudice, The Awakening, The Bluest Eye*. Thank you, the girls say when the dads hand them the money. No problem, the girls say. Anytime.

THE DADS DRIVE the girls home. Always, the dads drive. The dads turn the radio up. The dads change the station. The dads say, Do you like Vampire Weekend? The dads change the station again. The dads say, This one's an oldie. The dads say, I think I danced to this song at my prom. The dads say, You ever listen to the Velvet Underground? Or the dads turn off the radio. The dads don't want to be judged.

The dads don't know that the girls have already found the photos. The girls have spotted the DVDs. The girls have seen the websites. The girls have ransacked the history folders, the search terms, the cookies the dads didn't know how to erase.

The dads say, You know, I played football in high school. The dads say, Marching band was a big deal at my school. The dads say, All the kids in drama club were gay. The dads ask, Didn't you go to France last summer? The dads say, God, that would be nice. The dads say, I had a friend who spent a semester in France. The dads say, I hear every beach is a topless beach.

THE GIRLS ANSWER politely. The girls are good at talking to dads, talking to moms, talking to adults. The girls will be visiting colleges soon, where they will be interviewed by other moms, other dads. The girls know it's important to practice. Or the girls sit in silence. The girls stare at the road. The girls stare at their phones. The girls answer in single-syllable words: *Yeah. I guess so. I don't know.*

The girls like the kids of the dads and the moms. The girls read them stories. The girls are good at playing make-believe. The girls give horseback rides. The girls play Power Rangers. The girls play fairy princesses. The girls let the kids braid their hair. But the parents? The girls think the parents are almost as bad as the teachers. Almost.

THE DADS SAY, College applications, huh? The dads say, They really are the best years of your life. Or the dads say, Where you go to college doesn't matter, it's where you go to grad school that matters.

Or the dads sit in silence. The dads stare at the road.

THE GIRLS TEXT. They text their mothers, *On the way home.* They text their friends, *B there in 10.* They text their friends, *Marnie is such a beeyotch.* They text their friends, *Im on the drive . . . ugh.* They text their friends, *Somebody got his drink on.* They text boys, *We were so close to being bustedddddd!!!!!* They text boys, *I told u they come home earrrrrrrrrly.* They text boys, *There wont b a next time.*

THE MOMS CLEAN the kitchen. The moms check their e-mail. The moms straighten up the couch. The moms find the girls' earrings under the cushions. Hmm. The moms are going to have to talk to the girls, and to the girls' parents. Or the moms will say nothing, because the moms will think about when they were the girls, dating boys who were not the dads. The moms think about good boyfriends, bad boyfriends.

The moms wonder if the girls snoop. In the bedrooms, in the closets, in the bedside tables, in the bathrooms. When the moms were girls themselves, watching other kids, they always snooped.

The moms wash their faces. The moms put on T-shirts, the moms put on pajamas, the moms put on flannel nightgowns. The moms fall asleep before the dads have returned from the drive. Or the moms stay up. The moms read the book club's next pick. Or the moms wait in bed naked, to surprise the dads. The moms hear the cars in the driveway. The moms think again about when they were the girls, and *ugh,* the drive.

THE DADS SIT in the cars, waiting for the end of "Tenth Avenue Freeze-Out" or "Jack and Diane" or "Smells Like Teen Spirit." The dads haven't heard this song in years. The dads are tired.

The dads are whipped. The dads had one too many. The dads really should *not* have been driving. The dads stand in the driveway. They wait before going inside. The dads look at the stars, and every pinprick of light could be a sun surrounded by strange worlds full of dads, moms, girls, kids.

Henry and His Brother

His brother

Henry, he's a romantic. You give him hay and he spins it into gold; you show him an alley reeking of piss and horse shit from the last hansom-cab stable in the city, with the El hammering the tracks so loud you can feel it in your teeth, and he treats it like some kind of Shangri-La. It's fairyland, which I guess it is, if you want to be funny about it. But what does that make me? Some kind of chain-smoking Peter Pan? A big white rabbit stalking a sexed-up Alice? I'm the guy that tails him there night after night, and I stand on the corner and I wait for him to get what he needs and the whole time I'm praying this isn't the night he gets busted by the cops or worked over by some bruiser or else jumped by kids so goddamn scared of their own need that they kick the shit out of some guy doing exactly what they want most. But this is what brothers do for brothers. It's an unwritten rule, I'll be the first to admit that, though I'll bet there are plenty of brothers who'd say that it isn't a rule at all—written, unwritten, or tattooed in green ink on the soles of your feet. Now, where the hell did I get that one, right? Too much time with Henry, that's what that is.

Henry

Of course I know he's there. I could tell him not to follow me—to mind his own business—but following me has become his business. I never thought of him as the nurturing type. My brother is more Grant Park pigeon than mother hen, but right now he needs to think he's taking care of me, if that's what he's doing out there. I worry about him, though. The whole neighborhood is one big social experiment gone awry. Why else would you cram together a comedy club catering to the suburban-bachelorette-party circuit; a run-down peep show hawking damp, smudgy magazines to satisfy every dank, smutty fetish; a Mobbed-up restaurant surrounded by a phalanx of darkly idling town cars; the city's only upscale gay-porn cinema (may I direct your attention to the single tumescent orchid in the front window?); and then the source of my fascination and my brother's quiet consternation: the Near North Side's premier no-names-no-faces under-the-tracks cruising spot? And let us not forget the scowling, bruised-brick housing project two blocks to the west, the soaring lakeside condos two blocks to the east, and the alleyways and their blank-eyed garage doors gauded up in gang tags—crowns and eyes, bloated numbers and shivering letters code-talking boasts and threats known only to the initiated. And of course there's also the clopping of hooves against asphalt as the horses bring their carriages home for the night, lending the scene a Dickensian flair, if Dickens hadn't been such a prude about what really happened after lights-out in the workhouse. You take all of this and then compose as a sound track the throaty hum of the bells from the Church of St. Michael, God's own general in the war against Satan.

My brother must get mugged and heckled and threatened, hit up for money and asked to buy drugs or rent bodies, but he never says a word to me about it. Well, now it's his turn to keep secrets. My days in that line of work have ended.

Henry's brother again

I do this for my brother because for a long time I didn't do shit for him. I watched him sinking under the weight of God knows what and I never tried to lighten his load. He was a moper, a sad sack, a bookworm, and that's just how it was. He thought he was good for nothing, and who was I to argue? That's what kind of a brother I was. So one day he drank about a gallon of Sterno, and when they called me from the hospital I thought for sure he was dead. When I got to the hospital and saw him lying there, it was typical me: I laid into him about what a dumbshit he was and what was he trying to pull with a stunt like this and thank God Mom and Dad didn't live to see this, and I'll tell you, he went to fucking pieces. Tears like you've never seen, and the nurse came in to tell us to quiet down and did she need to call security and Henry's crying and then I'm crying because it hits me smack in the face that this is my brother. This is Henry. And I love the son of a bitch like he's the last good thing on the planet. Really. I mean, what else did I have? Joanne had left me and Mom and Dad had passed and it was just us, and I came this close to losing him. Without Henry I'm alone in this world, and I'll admit it, I'm not big enough to face that.

I moved him in with me when he got out of the hospital and after a week of quiet nights he told me why he did it, what brought it all on, and let me tell you, there were plenty more tears. I was ready to put his ass right back on the street. Return to sender, right? But I saw myself back in that hospital room crying my goddamn eyes out and I didn't want to lose him twice.

Henry has something he would like to clear up

About the Sterno, which I'm sure he has mentioned. There was a lot going on at the time. Living one life is hard enough. Living two was, I found out, more than I could handle. And when things went sour in the life I kept secret from my family—by which I mean my real life, the one that mattered more to me—I had only the pretend life to shore me up. Which became like hanging a lead vest on a paper doll. And it wasn't just Sterno, although that seems to be the part he has fixated on. The plan was half a bottle of Oxy and a pitcher of sangria, but right at the last minute—afraid that a cocktail of pharmaceuticals, alcohol, and fresh fruit wouldn't do the trick—I larded the sangria with half a dozen cans of Sterno. It was supposed to be for a party that had never been thrown, which was part of the original problem. Anyhow, it was under the sink. It was close at hand. I didn't realize at the time that what I had concocted was a magic potion that would allow me, after some effort, to live one life rather than two. It was at my brother's apartment that I opened up to him. I figured that I had burned down one life and now I would burn down the other and see if anything survived. I knew that he hadn't had an easy go of it either. Our parents, whom he had always been close to, had lived just long enough to see his own marriage succumb, and when all the drama with me started, his divorce wasn't even a year old. So we had both seen our share of wreckage, and after tears and words that didn't come easily in a family raised, as they say, with the good grace to conceal virtually everything from one another, what was left standing was me and him. I can't say we were transformed into creatures breathing nothing but the pure air of complete honesty. Have I mentioned that he follows me at night and stakes out a street corner without, he believes, my knowledge? But right now he needs someone to protect, and without that mission I fear he will crack up, like I did, and that his crack-up won't result in a magic potion but instead the blunt reality of a hole in the head or a rope around the neck. So this, my feigned ignorance, is a gift I can give to him, and from that comes a gift I can give myself: the continued presence in this world of one person who loves me.

Still, there's something Henry's brother wonders about

There was this guy he was with, I know that now, and they had a big brouhaha and the guy walked out on him for good. This came after years of Henry being alone. Most of the time alone-alone, just Henry waking up in his cold bed, sulking off to work, eating in front of the TV or going out to some twenty-four-hour place like the Golden Apple, party of one, which can make you feel worse because when you're sitting alone, the whole world looks like it's a two-top. Trust me on that one. But I'd also seen Henry alone-together, even if I didn't know it at the time. For a while he dated these women. I met some of them over the years, and what I'd always thought was *Man, does he have lousy taste in ladies.* Don't get me wrong, it wasn't like he always had a woman on his arm. He averaged about one a year, and the whole lot of them were sour-faced, mousy, sexless, and angry. Not all of them, but if you mixed up those words in a hat, you could have pulled out two or three to fit any of the women who passed through his life. The thing was, he made sure to bring each one around to meet me and Joanne or else to dinner at Mom and Dad's. He was the one who'd set it up; it wasn't like we were forcing him to parade around with his latest conquest. But then through the whole visit he'd look glum, like he was embarrassed to be sitting next to his latest lady friend. I thought, *Jeez, what does he see in these girls?* But at the same time I had to admit that they might be the best he could do, because Henry himself could be pretty goddamn sour-faced, and at his worst he could be a moody little SOB. I just chalked it up to bad taste or bad luck, and sooner or later the two of them would make each other miserable and one or the other would end it and after six months or a year he'd move on to his next lousy girlfriend.

How clueless was I that I never caught on? I think Joanne might have figured it out, but she never came right out and said it. Back when we were first together, or even during the first five years or so that we were married, I probably would've laughed it off, maybe said he *should* give the boys a try because it sure wasn't working out with the ladies. But if she'd've said anything like that in the last years, I don't think I would've taken it as a joke. I'd've probably gone off on her, you know? Just Joanne looking for another way to take a poke at me. Again, typical me. I would've said, *Yeah, I get it: I'm an asshole, my parents are always on your back about not having kids, and on top of it all, my brother's a fag. Is that the latest? Am I hearing that right?*

So anyway, there was Henry, and either he was trying to put on a show or else he was working hard to convince himself of something that just wasn't true. And it made him miserable, and that made these women miserable too. I don't think he meant to do that, but it's got to tear you up to love someone who won't or can't love you back. Or want to love someone but know that you can't. That you're just not built for it. Still, there's one thing that I've got to wonder about: It's not like things magically got better when he was with a guy. All this business that landed him in the hospital—that was over a guy. I'd like to think that with a guy, Henry would be different: looser, freer, happier. But maybe I've got it all wrong. Maybe he was just as glum and hard to be with. Maybe that's what pushed him over the edge, that he finally gave it a try, and he realized that it didn't matter who he was with. He was what he was. Maybe Henry isn't built for relationships of any kind, and he knows that, which is why he goes under the tracks. Five or ten minutes isn't much time to invest in anyone, and how bad can you feel if it doesn't turn out like you hoped? It's the years invested in loving another person, or trying to love them as best you can, that can turn your heart to stone and drag you down, deeper than you ever thought you could go.

Henry has something to say, in the interest of balance

He took me in, but I can't say it was a comfortable fit. I was a wreck, I won't deny that, but he wasn't exactly Gibraltar. When Joanne left him, my first thought was *Good riddance.* No, that's not exactly it. The first thing I thought was *Ding-dong, the witch is dead,* but I kept that to myself. When you're trying to throw yourself and your family and a city of three million off the scent of your shameful, hell-courting, man-loving ways, you keep the *Wizard of Oz* references to a minimum. I had always thought Joanne was a hen who pecked and pecked in search of some seed of fulfillment she would never find. Not that I saw him as the cock of the walk, but there they were—birds of a feather, stuck together. That's the picture I had developed, without much thought or insight, during my limited contact with them— limited, I'll admit, to the few holiday dinners I was unable to avoid despite tales of office emergencies that required my imme- diate attention or of the weddings of close friends I could not miss. You would be shocked at the number of Christmas Eve and Thanksgiving-weekend weddings I claimed to attend, how many dear college chums I said had chosen me as their best man just so I could deliver one of my famous tear-jerking, marriage-launching toasts.

God, where was I? Birds of a feather, which was a cruel thing to say about my own brother, given my low opinion of his wife. But it was also a terrible thing to say about Joanne. To me, she was always just my brother's wife. I suppose I could have made an ally of her, someone from outside the family who might have seen into my heart and taken my side in the inevitable blowup—assuming that I had ever been brave and honest enough to take that step. From the beginning I had the niggling suspicion that Joanne might have been just a bit more perceptive than my brother or my parents, but she was never what you would call warm, so who's to say she wouldn't have been the worst about it? I'll never know, and that's my fault, my loss. I never made the effort to get to know her as anything more than a category—the Wife, the In-Law. And maybe I was never any more to her than the Brother, the confirmation that whatever blank spots and broken pieces she found in her husband weren't just personal failings but hardwired into him by his screwy family.

It would be arrogant for me to think that I could be such a master of deceit and yet believe that my brother kept no secrets from his wife. I don't imagine his secrets were the same as mine, but if he was half as closed off as I was, that would have been enough to shut Joanne out of his life. What I saw as a harpy's talons lashing his lazy but undeserving hide may have been a desperate woman clawing at the door that once opened onto love and was now closing her into a dark cell with nothing to keep her company but her severed heart. She knew it would only get worse, so she scabbed over the raw, hot wound and met the world armored by her anger. I have to give her credit for that. I've certainly never learned how to do it.

Back to that first night

That first night, I got home before he did. He'd taken a roundabout way to get there and when he came out from the tracks, I hightailed it back to the apartment. I was sure it was drugs. What else could he be doing for ten minutes, in the dark, in a neighborhood like that? So I was sure it was drugs, but what do I know? Never inhaled, right? So he gets back to the apartment and I say, *Did you get some air?* and he says, *Yeah, I got plenty*. And I say, *Did you get anything else?* and he just stares at me. And I go, *Give me the drugs, Henry*. And he looks confused, and then he smiles, and he starts laughing. Laughing like I've never heard him laugh before. Like not since we were kids, and even then it happened only once, maybe twice. Laughing like I'd told the funniest joke in the world, so funny that it just might kill him.

And again with the first night

I don't know what possessed me that first night. Maybe I *was* possessed. That's an explanation my parents could have swallowed, if all of this had come to light when they were still alive. We were raised in the old school—not just Catholic, but Polish Catholic. A full calendar of holy days to be observed, a pantheon of saints to appease, and the Virgin Mary's tender embrace always just out of reach. When the model family is a virginal mother, a son who walks on water, and a father figure who puts up with all of this sexless perfection without complaint—well, it's bound to make you feel dysfunctional, even if your family isn't marbled with guilt and disappointment.

Do you see where my mind goes? I start trying to explain how I ended up beneath the tracks and the first place I go is the Blessed Virgin. I'll have to tell my shrink about that.

That first night, I just needed to get out. Out of the apartment. Out of myself. Out. It was nine or ten and it was fall—we had just set the clocks back and it was getting dark early, which only made the nights longer. I pulled on a jacket and before my brother could say anything I told him, *I need some air,* and he said, *Do you think that's such a good idea?* And I said, *I think it's a great idea.* I must have sounded crazy, which technically I probably was, if *crazy* is a technical term. See, another thing to ask the shrink.

So I was out the door and the truth is I didn't know where I was going, but after two blocks, with my breath steaming out of my mouth, I turned a corner and noticed my brother was tailing me.

He would have made the world's worst spy.

He must have thought I was going to pull a Virginia Woolf in the lake or jump from the top of the Sears Tower or make like

Anna Karenina and step in front of the Metra. But I'd tried that way of getting out and look how well that worked. Plus there's this: The lake is too cold, and if I were going to jump it would be from a Mies or the Hancock, and as for the Metra—death by commuter rail? That's where tragedy becomes farce.

I walked and my brother shadowed me, like this was all some game, some brotherly test of will. You want to see how far I'll go? Then I'll take you somewhere. I had heard about the tracks. My—the man I'd...I'd heard about what went on there from someone who knew. So that's where I went. That first night, my brother almost followed me in, then he realized that I'd stopped walking and he retreated to the corner.

Once I was there, it wasn't a game. Well, it was, but not a game between me and him. It was me versus me. I had dared myself in the kitchen. Now I dared myself again. There was a man there and my heart was racing and the air was cold and the train was pounding overhead and the wheels screamed and there were bright blue sparks and I just thought, *Yes.*

Henry's brother has one last thing to add

I like to go to the Field Museum on my lunch break when there's not so many tourists. Lots of screaming schoolkids, but what are you going to do? If I could go after hours, if I had my own key and could just let myself in late at night, I'd be the happiest guy, really. I bring this up because if you spend any time there, and you look at the totem poles and the bark huts and the canoes, you see that we adapt. People, I mean. Humans. We learn to do things that would have been hard to imagine right up until the time we actually do them. It's like when the ice age hits, and suddenly you've got to kill a big, hairy elephant with a sharp stick if you ever want to eat again. Or you've just walked from Asia to Alaska—which is already crazy enough—and then the ocean starts to rise, and you've got to figure out how to turn trees into boats so you can maybe someday get to a place where the weather is warm, and the bushes are full of fruit, and you can run around all day naked and happy. I tell you, it sounds crazy, but you do it because, really, what's the alternative?

My point is this: When all this with Henry started and I didn't totally blow my stack, I liked to pat myself on the back for being so open-minded. See how I've changed! Look at me adapt! But it wasn't ever my survival at stake, was it? All around Henry, the water was rising, and goddamn if he didn't find a way to get to higher ground.

And, finally, Henry

I love him, of course, but brotherly love doesn't explain what holds us together. I could say we're locked in some kind of mutual orbit, but that doesn't do it either—a vision of wandering bodies bound by unseen forces but separated by cold silence and vast distance. Our need for each other is messier than that. It's visceral, not celestial. I bleed, he bleeds, and maybe keeping each other close is the only way we know to keep pressure on the wound.

Salvage

Hunched in the bed of the pickup truck, freezing rain needling his face, Tommy Doyle had to admit that Iceland might not be such a great idea. He had spent all day wrestling three antique fireplace mantels out of an old mansion in Michigan City and into the back of the truck. It should have been a half-day job, but the old house didn't give up its treasures so easily, and by the time he and Wilkie left for Chicago, it was already dark. Though they'd managed to remove the mantels without a scratch on them, Tommy had gouged the meat of his thumb with a chisel. All the way back to Chicago, driving on the sleet-choked Skyway, his hand throbbed like a second heart beneath the makeshift bandage. When traffic ground to a stop, Tommy pulled off the Skyway—a bad idea, and yes, that's exactly what Wilkie had told him—and in search of a shortcut, he'd gotten lost in a tangle of bombed-out blocks in South Chicago. If that wasn't bad enough, one corner of the tarp over the bed of the truck had blown loose and the mantels were getting drenched. Fixing it should have taken just a second, but after ten minutes of picking with his teeth and bitten-down fingernails at the soaked twine knots, he felt like the bulging disk in his back and the knife-edge of the wind were playing rock-paper-scissors to decide which would knock him on his ass once and for all.

To the east, thick clouds rode low over Lake Michigan. Between him and the lake was the site once occupied by the South Works steel mill. The empty land, the whitecaps on the lake, and the charcoal sky were a dead ringer for the pictures of Iceland in the travel books Tommy had bought last fall. He had imagined the island as a place where it was just you and the elements and no one around to hassle you. But as he re-tied the last knot and blew uselessly on his cramped fingers, he considered that the wild frontier of his imagination, his refuge in the North Atlantic, might be just as cold and nasty as Chicago.

Through the back window of the cab, he could see Wilkie nodding off in the passenger seat. He was an old guy—sixty, maybe seventy—and he was slow as hell, but he was careful, and Tommy had never once heard him complain. Which was probably why Hank, the owner of the architectural-salvage company where they both worked, always called him for day-labor jobs. That and the fact that Wilkie knew the city like he knew his own bedroom. There wasn't a block in Chicago where he hadn't run a brick-salvage crew, cleaning and stacking thousands of bricks a day with nothing more than claw hammers and wooden pallets.

Back in the truck, Tommy cranked up the heat, his hands

over the vents. "I'd better check in with Hank," he said to Wilkie. "He's probably been throwing a shit-fit wondering where we are."

"Sounds like a good reason not to call him," Wilkie said, but as Tommy reached for his phone, he saw that it had gone dead, and the charger was nowhere to be found.

Down a side street, the rotting shells of warehouses loomed. Farther down the block glowed a loop of blue neon and an Old Style sign swaying on two rusty chains. Tommy asked Wilkie if he thought the bar might have a pay phone, but Wilkie just shrugged, like if Tommy was really going to call Hank, then Wilkie wanted no part of it.

Tommy parked in front of the bar and told Wilkie he'd be back in a minute. As he pushed through the metal front door, he was met by a blast of music shimmering with rapid-fire brass. There were a dozen men in the room, in baseball caps and faded canvas jackets, who looked like the crew at Tommy's last job—Central Americans who would do any task as long as the company didn't look too hard at their Social Security numbers. Tommy caught the eye of the bartender and pressed his hand to his head, thumb and pinkie extended. The bartender, a young guy with a thick ponytail, gestured toward a hallway at the back of the room. Few heads turned his way as he lumbered through the bar.

There was a pay phone near the men's room and as soon as Hank picked up, it was clear that Tommy hadn't done himself any favors by calling. Hank had a buyer coming first thing Monday morning to look at the mantels, and if there was so much as a single mark on the wood, he told Tommy, "It's coming out of your ass, kid." Hank was always calling him a kid, as in "this kid wouldn't know Frank Lloyd Wright from the Wright brothers," but Tommy didn't feel like a kid, not with his aching back and his frozen hands. He was twenty-eight with a body going on eighty-eight.

He hung up the phone and found Wilkie sitting at the bar, a bottle of beer in front of him and another on the bar waiting for Tommy. The first beer only made him thirstier but the second went down easy, in a few long pulls at the bottle. When the bartender gave him the third, he got the side-eye from Wilkie, but Tommy didn't care. He could knock back a twelve-pack of the cheap stuff and barely feel it, though the jumpy twitch that had sent him off the Skyway had finally subsided, reduced to a numb crackle along his nerves. He held the cold bottle against his bandaged hand, the chill answered by a sharp throb. His last two Vicodin were in his pocket but he didn't want to burn them just yet; he'd need them after the mantels were unloaded and the job was done.

Beer in his hand, Tommy took his first good look around the room. He hadn't noticed when he came in, but the place had been something once. Maybe the taproom of a union hall or a fraternal lodge—the Secret Order of Big Shots and Lowlifes, a blanket term his father used for the Masons, Elks, and other clubs where men gathered to drink cheap beer and wear funny hats. Dark wainscoting girdled the walls; pressed tin covered the ceiling. The paint was flecked and peeling, but the pattern on the tin was fancier than he would have expected to see in a bar on the roughed-up fringes of South Chicago. Lots of bars from the first half of the century had tin ceilings, he had learned in his time working for Hank, but most used basic patterns: grids, diagonal lines, an occasional rosette. The design above the faded felt of the pool table and the scattering of Mexican soccer posters was more elaborate, with curlicue vines connecting ripe fleurs-de-lis. Hank could probably get a decent price for the ceiling from one of the restaurant designers who bought from him, but it would be a pain in the ass to get the pieces down. Even with scaffolding set up, it was overhead work, and that meant dead arms, knotted shoulders, and a face full of lead paint.

He was about to say something to Wilkie about the ceiling when he looked above the bar mirror and his jaw went slack. Whoever had spent the extra nickel per square yard on the tin ceiling had spent a whole lot more on the back bar. It sprawled against the wall, thirty feet from end to end, its massive central arch topped by a crown molding as thick as a wedding cake.

"Pretty nice, huh?" Tommy said, pointing from one end to the other.

"Been looking at it this whole time," Wilkie said. "Craftsmanship. That's what you see there."

"What do you think Hank could get for something like that?" Tommy had in mind a couple grand, easy.

"Don't know," Wilkie said. "Eight, maybe ten thousand. Don't see too many like that."

Tommy whistled. For the first time, he started to think tonight might not be a total waste. On Monday, he would let Hank lay into him about being late and allowing his phone to die, and then he'd hit him with the news that he'd found a kick-ass bar, an old one, a goddamn antique, and that would get Hank's attention. Hank could be a real prick, but if you had something he wanted, he'd shut up and get down to business. From his jacket pocket, Tommy unfolded one of the flyers that Hank used to market his architectural-salvage business. Below the headline WE BUY BARS!!! was a collage of antique bars—deco, English pub, Mission, double-arch, and a massive single-arch like the one that loomed against the wall. HANK'S ARTIFACTS, the phone number, and WE WILL PAY YOU CASH—CALL TODAY!!! ran along the bottom of the page.

Tommy jotted his name next to the phone number and called the bartender over. He handed him the flyer and said, "For the boss." And then, in his job-site Spanish, he added, *"Para el jefe."*

Tommy was feeling pretty pleased with himself. He slid off his stool and straightened up, palms at the base of his spine the way the physical therapist had shown him. "What do you think Hank'll give us for finding it?" he said to Wilkie. He was already imagining a cut of the sale. A commission. He deserved one for finding a bar like this.

"I guess it would be an all-day job," Wilkie said. "Take it apart. Get it wrapped right. Get it on the truck." He finished his beer, then picked up a napkin from a stack behind the bar and patted his lips. "So figure whatever you make for a day's work, that's what Hank'll give you."

"You don't think we'll get a bonus for this?" Tommy caught himself shouting and dropped his voice to a sharp whisper. "Seriously, don't we deserve a finder's fee?"

Wilkie chuckled. "Are we talking about what we deserve or what we gonna get?" He folded the napkin and put it under his bottle. "Now it's time for you to get this old man home. I can't be out drinking with young folks on a Saturday night. What's my wife gonna think?"

Tommy dropped Wilkie along a row of squat bungalows and two-flats on the South Side, in Englewood, then picked his way back toward the expressway. It was after ten when he lugged the last of the mantels into the shop, a third-floor loft west of the Loop that was packed with the spoils of hundreds of condemned properties. Brass chandeliers, entryway lanterns, and Holophane lights crowded the ceiling. Stations of the Cross hung along one wall, flanked by wrought-iron window grilles from the old state mental hospital. In one corner, a set of stained-glass windows illustrated Mother Goose rhymes; in another, a forest of fluted wooden columns slumped against the wall. Terra-cotta urns and stern-eyed busts from an old bank in Milwaukee were piled in the center of the room.

There was no sign of Hank or of the three weeks' pay Tommy was still owed. He had planned on catching up with some buddies for drinks, but it had been a long day, everything ached, and paying for beers with Wilkie had practically cleaned him out. He plopped himself into Hank's overstuffed desk chair, plugged in his phone, and punched his way through texts and voice mails: four calls from Hank (*Where the hell are you?*), one from his mother (*Don't forget about church on Sunday*), one about the rent he still hadn't paid (*Come on, man, it's been, like, three months*), and a text from a waitress canceling a date he was too broke to keep anyway (*sry! cu ltr*).

Everything hurt. His back, his hand, his head. He fished the last two Vicodin out of the bottle in his jacket pocket and swallowed them dry. While he waited for them to kick in, he leafed through the stack of catalogs from the big auction houses in Atlanta that Hank kept on his desk.

Hank had auction catalogs going back five or six years, with the prices paid for every marble angel and spitting-dolphin fountain written next to the pictures. Tommy often flipped through the pages when Hank wasn't around and thought about what it would be like to be one of those people who paid thousands of dollars to decorate their gardens with gargoyles from old churches or who outfitted their billiards rooms with light fixtures from old English pubs. He figured you had to be pretty loaded just to *have* a billiards room, forget about a garden big enough for gargoyles.

He was halfway through last spring's catalog when he saw the Del Monte. *Widely regarded as the finest bar ever produced,* the caption read, *the Del Monte was Brunswick's top-of-the-line offering and is the most prized of all the turn-of-the-century back bars.* The one in the catalog was cleaned up—rich cherry wood with brass fixtures—but it was the same bar he had seen that night. The same center arch, the same columns, the same fat wedge of molding along the top. Scrawled beneath the picture was the final hammer price: *$40,000.*

"Holy shit," he said to the empty office. "Holy. Fucking. Shit." The Del Monte was the kind of home run Hank hoped to hit every time he walked into some falling-down, boarded-up storefront. That was always where the best stuff was—the treasures that had survived because no one remembered that they had ever existed: the bronze chandelier lurking above the drop ceiling, the stained-glass windows bricked over when the Catholics moved to the suburbs and the Missionary Baptists moved in. Tommy had heard all of these stories, the legends of the salvage trade, during the days spent driving the city with Hank, and now he was at the center of a legend in the making: *Did you hear about that guy Doyle who found a Del Monte on the South Side?*

Just as quickly as the story started to take shape, though, another thought flashed through his head. He had finally found something rare and beautiful—*the finest bar ever produced*—but Wilkie was right: Hank wouldn't offer him a dime more than his wages for pulling out the bar and loading it on a truck. The Del Monte was the first piece of good luck he'd had in a long time, and there was nothing he could do but hand it over to Hank with the hope that a few crumbs would fall his way.

A YEAR AGO, Tommy had been working on an asbestos-abatement crew, making good money and picking up a fifty here and there from Hank for passing on leads about buildings coming up for demolition. Before any building came down, the asbestos had to be removed, which gave Tommy the inside track. Hank was a fixture around demolition sites, gabbing over a cup of coffee with the wreckers or barking out instructions to the gang of day laborers he hired for each job. He taught

Tommy what to look for on any job site—what was worth saving, what wasn't—and passed on a few crisp bills whenever one of Tommy's tips led to a good deal.

Then Tommy had his accident, slipping off a ladder while pulling fireproof ceiling tiles out of an elementary school. When the other guys on the crew helped him to his feet, he felt hot barbed wire whipping through his legs and coiling around his spine. He filed for workers' comp, but the company contested the claim—something about Tommy's drinking, as if coming to work with a hangover was a federal offense. While his case was being investigated, he needed a place where he could work off the books. Hank was happy to oblige. He preferred to deal in cash—no records, no taxes, no hassles—and for the first month it seemed like a good fit. Hank drove Tommy around the city scouting properties that were on the city demo list, bragging about his best finds and complaining about his ex-wife.

The first thing Tommy learned about the salvage business was that it was shady as hell. Sometimes the calls about an item up for sale came from a building owner, sometimes from the wreckers, sometimes from a building superintendent looking to make a few extra bucks. The rule on any job was to move fast and not attract too much attention. And half the time when Hank handed over a check, there wasn't even enough money in the account to cover it. He counted on lining up a buyer who would pay on delivery—often directly from the site where they had just removed the piece—and if all went well, the deposit would hit the account just before the withdrawal. Hank called it "brokering," because it was how you had to work when you were broke.

There was a lot of heavy lifting—taking down a limestone pediment, pulling pews from old churches—but it was a welcome break from asbestos removal, which was always indoors and most active during the hottest stretch of summer. On asbestos jobs, with his body stuffed into coveralls and a respirator clamped to his face, Tommy spent his days hauling bags full of waterlogged insulation to the dumpsters. Working in the summer heat, he would sweat through his clothes before the first morning break. On days when the boss or the city inspectors weren't on-site, he often stripped to shorts and a T-shirt, his thick limbs glazed with dust and matted fibers. He hated the feeling of always being so close to suffocation, but after eight years on the job, there wasn't anything else he could do that paid as well.

He wasn't making anything close to asbestos money working for Hank, who kept Tommy on the run hauling terra-cotta blocks around the shop and driving out to postage-stamp towns in central Illinois for pickups and drop-offs. Maybe he should have called it quits with Hank, and maybe, by January, he was healthy enough to return to asbestos work, but it wasn't clear if EnviroCorp would even take him back after the workers' comp thing, and besides, after years of working every shit job the company sent his way, he deserved a little paid vacation. And his back *did* hurt; he wasn't making it up. Every day as he drove home from Hank's, he gobbled painkillers—Vicodin when he could get it; handfuls of ibuprofen when he couldn't—and asked himself how much worse it had to hurt before he could get what he was owed.

TOMMY WOKE UP in his own bed on Sunday morning, but it was a mystery how he'd found his way back to his apartment, a glorified dorm room with bad plumbing and dingy white wall-to-wall carpet. He remembered the Vicodin and stopping at the twenty-four-hour Osco for a handful of vodka nips and some orange juice. He remembered the Del Monte and its price tag. And he remembered getting back in his car, but after that things got hazy. Now his head was throbbing, his back had tightened up, and his hand had left a bloody trace on the sheets. He stared across the room at a map of Iceland that he had found in a copy of *National Geographic* in the physical therapist's waiting room. He'd read the article from start to finish, then reread it at his next appointment. With the summer heat, the accident, and the haze of asbestos fibers still fresh in his mind, Iceland sounded like paradise: an island of hot tubs and glaciers, Vikings and all-night parties down the main drag of Reykjavík. When he finally got his workers' comp money, he promised himself he'd take a trip to Iceland to celebrate and maybe to get his head together. He had already gotten a Viking tattoo—a circle bristling with spokes and lines—modeled on a picture he'd seen in that same *National Geographic*. The magazine said it was a compass carved into boats to bring them home and inked onto the skin of the Norsemen to guide them from this world to the next, just in case the boats didn't make it back. So maybe he had the tattoo to thank for getting him home last night. If nothing else, the tattoo was supposed to remind him that Vikings took no shit from anyone, and as far as Tommy was concerned, he had been taking too much shit for too long.

But for now, there was more shit-taking on the way. His sister's new baby was being baptized after the 9:45 Mass in Orland Park, and one look at the clock told him that he was going to be late. His sister Kathleen lived in one of the fancier northwest suburbs but had decided to have the baptism at the church where they'd all grown up—and that meant the reception at their parents' house was sure to be a forced march down memory lane. And of course he'd have his parents to deal with: Mom full of questions, Dad full of opinions. It was too much on a Sunday morning.

When he rolled into the church—after the Mass but just in time for the baptism—his mother gave him a kiss and then leaned in close. "You don't look so good," she said.

"Nice to see you too," he said, wedging himself into the stiff wooden pew.

While the godparents took their places and his sister fidgeted with the laces on the baby's gown, Tommy gazed across the altar, contemplating a price for the pulpit, which was ringed with inlaid Gothic arches. He estimated how much he could get for the rose window above the choir loft and whether he would need ladders or a cherry picker to remove the panes of glass. As the priest asked the assembled if they rejected Satan and all his empty promises, Tommy calculated the value of the marble baptismal font, the pews, and the statues of the saints at the front of the church. Saints were easier to sell than crucifixes unless your buyer was another church. People liked having a saint in the garden, but it was only the collectors and cultists who asked about giant crucifixes; it was one thing to have Saint Francis smiling at you in the backyard, but few had the stomach for a bleeding Christ glowering in the living room. As candles were lit by the godparents, he wondered if the altar could be moved as a single piece or if it was bolted together and would have to be disassembled. From where he stood, he couldn't tell if it was solid wood or veneer; he'd need to take a look under the altar cloth to say for sure. Working for Hank had taught him which questions to ask, but he was stung by the certainty that he could never afford to do anything with the answers.

Tommy's sister was only a year older than he was, but suddenly, it seemed, all of her friends had acquired their own homes, jobs without name tags, spouses they'd met in college, fat-faced children—the whole package. The guys were already losing hair, packing on weight, dressing like their fathers. The girls—girls he had dated, girls he had ignored, girls he had never had a shot at—gained and lost baby weight, sold real estate, talked SoulCycle. For years, he had bragged about how little he had changed, how everyone else had sold out and settled down but he was still the same old Tommy Doyle. The Most Eligible Bachelor in Chicago, he'd once called himself. The King of Saturday Night, his father had said. It hadn't been a compliment, but what did Tommy care? His father hounded him all the time about dropping out of college, wasting his money living in the city—basically for doing anything that wouldn't lead to a house in the suburbs and summers in the Wisconsin Dells. Tommy hadn't let any of it change him. But lately being the same old Tommy was starting to feel like a curse he couldn't break.

Tommy promised his mother he would stop by their house for the reception, but almost as soon as he arrived, he retreated upstairs. In his old bedroom, the posters and team pictures from his years on varsity had been removed long ago, but one shelf still held his high-school trophies—football mostly, a few from baseball and wrestling—shiny sprayed-gold figures frozen in the moment of victory. In the bathroom medicine cabinet, Tommy found a two-year-old bottle of Percocet left over from his father's rotator-cuff surgery. Twenty or thirty pills rattled inside. It was the first good news of the day, and it was also classic Dad: he'd rather tough it out than take pain meds. Who needed pills anyway? Well, Tommy sure did. He thought about grabbing the whole bottle but he had no way to carry it that it wouldn't be obvious. Instead, he dumped half the pills into his hand and slid them into his pocket. He checked the bottle again and took out five or six more. He swallowed two and pocketed the rest. "Thanks, Dad," he said to the mirror.

He wanted to make a quick getaway—an Irish good-bye—but he had to wait at the top of the narrow stairs while someone else walked up. Just by the rhythm of the feet, he knew it was his father. The pills felt like a pocketful of gravel, and Tommy darted a look down to see if there was any way to tell that he had them. When his father reached the top, Tommy tried to step out of his way.

"Still working at that junk shop?" his father said.

"Artifacts, Dad. We call them artifacts."

He shrugged. "You can't be making much doing that."

"I'm doing okay," Tommy said.

His father shook his head, dismissing whatever nonsense Tommy was saying. "You need to get back to work—real work."

"As soon as my case—"

"Your case," he said, like it was part of some kid's make-believe story. "Look, at some point, you've got to stop looking for a hand-out and man up."

He'd heard this talk—this lecture—half a dozen times since he'd gotten hurt. About how when life knocks you down, you've got to get up. About taking responsibility. About manning up. Tommy buried his hands in his pockets and acted like he was listening closely, giving his dad his full attention. But what he was thinking about was the Percocet and how he should have taken one or two more when he was in the bathroom, when he'd had his chance.

"Dad," Tommy said, needing to put a stop to his father's talking. There was so much noise coming from downstairs, and the hallway was too small for the two of them, and Tommy wanted a drink, and his back was starting to send jabs of pain down his legs. He needed something to say, even if it was just *See you later,* to keep his father from starting up again. "Look, I've got something in the works," he said. "Something big, okay? I found a bar that every dealer in the country is going to want."

His father sighed—exasperated, disappointed, or just bored. It was hard to tell the difference. "That's great for what's-his-name," he said, "but I don't see—"

"It's not Hank's deal," Tommy said. "It's mine. I'm running it myself."

His father shook his head, like Tommy still didn't get it. His case. His deal. But Tommy plowed ahead, laying one detail on top of another: the Del Monte, the names of auction houses and West Coast buyers, the specifics of hiring a crew, bits and pieces of architectural history that he'd picked up around the shop. Maybe his father wouldn't believe a word of it, but the more Tommy spoke, the more he convinced himself that he could do it. Half of Hank's sales were brokered—and now Tommy was going to broker the shit out of the Del Monte. He still needed to buy the bar, but that would come—of course it would. He could offer ten thousand and still make a decent profit. He didn't see how the bar's owner could possibly turn down ten thousand dollars. He liked the sound of the deal so much that he told the story twice more on the way out of the house, once to Kathleen's husband, who'd never thought much of Tommy, and once to his mother, so she wouldn't worry so much. When he left the party, it wasn't because he felt like he was drowning in a sea of people happier and better off than he was. He was leaving because he had business to take care of.

DRIVING AWAY FROM his parents' house, he was so sure that he could close the deal that he allowed himself to think about what would come next. He wouldn't make a fortune, but it would be enough to settle up with his landlord and launch himself into a new apartment. Enough to catch up on his car payments. Enough to hire a better lawyer for his case or just say to hell with EnviroCorp and start over somewhere else. It was enough to tell Hank to go fuck himself the next time he ordered him to drive halfway across the state to pick up a load of junk. And it was enough for a ticket to Iceland, where no one knew the old Tommy Doyle, where maybe his bad luck wouldn't follow him, and where he would hike the glaciers and soak in the hot springs and feel the wasted years boil out of him.

But the farther he drove from his parents and his big talk about the Del Monte, the more he wavered. He had no bar and no buyer. And maybe the Del Monte hadn't been as nice as he remembered—and maybe it wasn't a Del Monte at all. He didn't even know where the bar was—not exactly. It had been dark and late when he'd found it and he'd been buzzed and exhausted by the time he left. He remembered a flash of neon, an Old Style sign—but that described half the dive bars in the city. He hoped that the same sense memory that had guided him home last night would get him back to the bar, but after an hour of driving up and down the streets and alleys of South Chicago, he was jittery and impatient. He stopped at a convenience store for a tall can of beer and cracked it open in his car. After a few deep slugs from the can, he washed down another pill from his parents' house. He knew what too much time behind the wheel could do to his back and he needed to stay loose.

The car moved and he moved with it. He knew the city well enough that he didn't have to think much when he was driving, but lately he had a hard time telling if he was the driver or a passenger. It seemed as if the car went where it wanted, and the wheel and the pedals just gave him something to do.

He followed the low concrete barrier and tall chain-link fence that marked the perimeter of the steel mill's site, but all he saw were empty lots broken by rows of small houses. He passed a school and a playground, crossed the Metra tracks and then crossed them again, but none of it looked familiar. He tried coming at the neighborhood from the Skyway, re-creating last night's path, but he found himself rolling down the same vacant streets, the same narrow alleys. He had been driving for hours and he hadn't gotten anywhere. He was sick to his stomach and the blood was pounding in his temples; this was classic Tommy Doyle, wasn't it? *Did you hear about that Doyle kid? Said he found a Del Monte and then couldn't remember where it was!*

He drove out of South Chicago and back to Englewood. Wilkie's neighborhood was a tidy street of brick houses fronted by stripped trees that in the summer would shade the sidewalks and trimmed lawns. Tommy remembered that Wilkie's house was next door to a place that still hadn't taken down its Christmas decorations; a sign in that yard announced, in spangled letters, JESUS IS THE REASON FOR THE SEASON. He parked out front, knocked, and stood back from the door. When Wilkie answered, he looked Tommy up and down as if he'd just been handed a screwdriver to do a hammer's job. His face was smooth; the skin practically shone. It was the first time Tommy could remember seeing him without a few days' growth on his cheeks.

Tommy jumped right in, as if they were already in the middle of a conversation. "Wilkie, you saw that bar. It's nice, right? I mean, nice enough that somebody would pay a lot for it."

Wilkie stepped forward, leaving the door open just a crack behind him. "What's this all about? Because I'm about to sit down for my supper."

Tommy had started off all wrong, and he could feel the pressure building inside him. He knew that if he kept talking, he'd soon be ranting on the man's front steps. "Don't tell Hank about it, okay?" he finally said. "You never saw it. It doesn't exist."

Wilkie looked out at the street, then back over his shoulder into the house. From inside came the sound of silverware and plates. The warm smell of people and food. "You okay, Tommy?"

Tommy forced a smile. "Yeah, I'm cool."

"I didn't ask if you were cool."

Tommy exhaled, his ragged breath visible in the air. He had come to Wilkie for some kind of assurance about the bar, but what he really wanted to know was if he had already passed the point of no return, after which nothing would ever truly work out the way he wanted it to. When had it happened? Was it when he went to work for Hank? Or before that? Maybe filing the workers' comp claim. Or not getting a tighter grip on the ladder on the day of the accident. Or, to take it all the way back, partying his way out of college. Whatever the case, it was a litany of fuckups. But was he *fucked*—permanently and irrevocably? If part of life was paying his dues, well, he was willing to bust his ass before things really started to click. But what if all he ever did was pay and pay, and he never got anything in return?

Wilkie stood there with his shoulders hunched against the mounting cold, but what had Tommy expected him to say? There wasn't anyone who could tell him how to pull out of this tailspin or guarantee that this time was just a rough patch required for the sweet life that would inevitably follow.

"Sorry to interrupt your dinner," Tommy said. "I guess I'll see you later."

"I guess you will," Wilkie said.

MONDAY MORNING FOUND him in the same shabby apartment, his legs numb, his head like a cloud of static, his insides raw as a rusty can. It was the same as every morning, and he was in no rush to get to work. Either Hank had sold the mantels and Tommy would have to reload them for delivery or the buyer had backed out and Hank would be in a foul mood.

Tommy arrived in the shop just after noon and found Hank sitting at his desk with a paper bag mottled with grease and ketchup stains.

"Well, look who's finally up," Hank said. "You've got work to do, kid."

Tommy mumbled something about a doctor's appointment, as if Hank cared. Hangover, doctor's appointment, death in the family—it would have been the same to Hank. Hank shrugged and leaned back in his chair, picking french fries from the bag one at a time. "Hey, some guy called for you. Mexican guy, I think." Hank pointed with a fry at a pink WHILE YOU WERE OUT note. In thick black marker, he had written, *LAZARO—BAR* followed by an out-of-town cell phone number.

A surge of acid raced up Tommy's throat as he remembered the flyer he'd left at the bar on Saturday night. *Para el jefe,* he'd told the bartender, and it looked like this Lazaro was El Jefe. He swallowed hard and snatched the note from the desk. "Thanks," he said. "I got it."

"So what's the story?" Hank said. "This guy's got a bar?"

"It's just that place I called from Saturday night."

Hank wiped his fingers on the bag. "Let's see what he's got."

Tommy eased himself down into a chair. "That's all right. I'll handle it."

"You'll handle it? What does that mean?"

Tommy shrugged. "It means I'll handle it."

"Don't go holding out on me. If you found a bar on my time, then it's my deal."

"Hank, there's no deal," Tommy said. "It's just some bullshit bar."

"That's really not your call, is it?"

Tommy tipped his face to the ceiling and rubbed his eyes with his hands, like a man waking up from a long sleep. "Just mind your own business, okay?"

"This is my fucking business, you little shit. You're out there in my truck, working for me, and you're going to tell me that it's not my business?"

"You pay me for pickups and drop-offs," Tommy said. "Hell, you don't even pay me for doing that. But what I do on my time is my business."

"Tell me where it is, you son of a bitch!" Hank said as he stabbed his finger at Tommy. The two of them were facing each other in the small office, ten feet and a wastebasket between them. "You don't get to decide what's your business. Now where the fuck is it?" Hank's face was livid, his outstretched hand rigid as a pair of scissors.

Tommy could still turn this whole thing into a joke. *I really had you going, didn't I? You should have seen your face.* He might even get some grudging credit from Hank for showing some balls or at least for finding an honest-to-God Del Monte. *You fucking kid. You lucky little bastard.* Hank would find the bar, and if he could work out a deal with this Lazaro, then the next time Tommy saw the Del Monte would be when Hank sent him to take it apart, wrap it up, and get it on the truck. Tommy must've been crazy for thinking he could put this deal together. He couldn't even remember where the bar was. It was all some stupid fantasy, wasn't it? But then he looked again at the pink slip of paper in his hand. There was nothing there but a name and a number.

"Fuck off," Tommy said. "It's mine."

Hank lurched out of his chair, but before he could take two steps Tommy was on his feet. He was a head taller than Hank, twenty years younger, and fifty pounds heavier. He squeezed the paper in his fist and shook it in Hank's face.

"I dare you," Tommy said. "I dare you."

Hank took a step back, feeling for the edge of his desk, and then smirked. "Wilkie!" he yelled. "Wilkie, get up here!"

Wilkie was at the back of the shop rewiring a set of brass sconces. Tommy could hear his footsteps approaching on the gritty concrete floor.

"I want you to see this," Hank said to Tommy. "And then I want you to get the fuck out of here."

Wilkie appeared at the door, a pair of pliers in one hand.

"That bar where you and Doyle stopped last Saturday—what kind of back bar did it have?"

"A nice one," Wilkie said. He rubbed his chin, still smooth from yesterday's shave.

"Oh yeah?" Hank said, looking directly at Tommy. "How nice?"

"Tommy here said it was nicer than anything he'd ever seen in the shop," Wilkie said.

Tommy tried to catch Wilkie's eye. When had he said that? And why was Wilkie making it worse? But Wilkie just gave him a nod of the head, like they'd spent hours trash-talking Hank's inventory.

"Oh, he did, did he?" Hank was loving this.

Tommy would have walked out and just kept on walking except that his legs were full of lead and his whole body felt like it was sinking into the floor.

"We figured it was worth a few thousand, easy," Wilkie said.

"So, Wilkie," Hank said, again looking straight at Tommy, "where's it at?"

Wilkie rubbed his chin again, chewed the inside of his cheek. "Thing is, I can't really say." He shook his head. "Tommy got us so turned around getting there that I didn't know which way was up. Then on the way home, I fell straight asleep."

"Wilkie," Hank sputtered. "What the fuck?"

"I suppose it was those beers Tommy bought me. He had to wake me up when he dropped me by my place." Wilkie laughed. "Dolores wasn't too happy about that. No sirree."

"Wilkie." Hank practically barked the word. "Are you shitting me?"

"I'm real sorry, Hank." Wilkie shook his head. "That sure

was a nice bar." He worked the pliers open and shut a couple of times. "Well, I gotta be getting back to those lights."

Hank's head looked like it was going to burst. He pulled a toothpick from between his teeth and whipped it across the room. "Get the fuck out of here!" he said to Tommy. "You're done. Do you hear me? You're done!"

DRIVING TO SOUTH Chicago, Tommy again had the feeling that the car was doing the work, that he was riding rather than driving. The whole way down, he hoped that Hank was right. He wanted to be done. Done with Hank, done with waiting on EnviroCorp, and done with being the same old Tommy Doyle.

It was the middle of the afternoon when he found the bar. He recognized the derelict warehouse down the street, the Old Style sign, the unlit neon in the window. The bar wasn't open for business and the iron lattice of the front door's security gate was padlocked. He took hold of the gate and gently rattled the bars as if to make sure it was no mirage. He wanted one look inside—proof that that he'd found something valuable—and that would be enough. If there was an honest-to-God Del Monte in there, then the stories he'd told at his parents' house would be at least half true. He had found a Del Monte, the best of its kind. He just didn't know how to do anything about it.

The second time he shook the bars, he gripped them harder and with both hands, trying to jar the gate loose from its hinges. The third time he gave it all he had, not just his own strength and weight, but his anger and frustration and disappointment and rage and humiliation and stubbornness and fury about his inability to make anything in his life—not one single thing—work out the way it was supposed to. He let loose a yell, a weight lifter's yell, a maniac's yell, and he rattled the bars and they shrieked metal on metal but they held firm.

When he released his grip, he was panting and his hands were speckled with rust. One was welted with thick red lines and the other was welted and bleeding and he felt the sting of the rust in his cut. His breath came in great heaves, and the tears in his eyes stung in the icy air.

The gate looked like a flimsy thing but he could not move it—and what if he could? The door behind it was a windowless slab of metal, meat-locker gray. Was he going to bust through that just to see if the Del Monte was real? He took two steps back, staggering, and his hot gaze fell on the window. Covered by its own smaller lattice of bars, it mirrored back the street. He couldn't make out anything behind the glass.

He stepped back to the edge of the crumbling curb, his breathing ragged and his hand throbbing. He reached down, picked up a fist-size piece of concrete, and hurled it at the window. His first toss pocked off the security bars and sprayed grit on the window, but the second chunk of rock and the third slipped through the gate and smashed the glass. He threw every piece of concrete he could pull from the curb—some the size of baseballs, some just a handful of buckshot. He threw it all, until his shoulders burned and shocks burst across the small of his back.

He knew that he'd gone too far, but he didn't see the point in stopping. Stopping meant that he'd have to figure out what to do next. As long as he was throwing rocks at the window, clearing it of glass, he didn't have to ask himself what came next.

Not until the police car arrived, and the cops started shouting, and Tommy kept throwing concrete, and the cops kept shouting, did he finally stagger back another step and sit heavily on the street. The police cuffed him and hauled him to his feet. In the back of the cruiser, his face slumped against the window and every part of his body aching, he watched the low sun throw sparks off the lake. It was time for whatever came next.

WHEN TOMMY FIRST tried to get sober, he talked in the meetings about the bar and Hank and his injury and Iceland and the chance to make twenty or thirty grand and how all of it had pushed him to lose control. He said that, as he was driven away from the bar, he imagined he wasn't in a police car moving north on Lake Shore Drive but in an airplane making its final approach to a faraway island of fire and ice. He said that he had left one life behind and was ready to start another.

Years later, in meetings in church basements and community centers, he would admit that that weekend was only the beginning of a long effort to get clean. In those early days, he still hadn't learned that no one owed him anything for the bad luck and the missteps that had derailed him. Or that pain wasn't some kind of token he could pile up and then cash in. Pain was only pain. He wanted those wasted years to count for something, but time only moved forward. And all he could do was make something of the days to come.

My Last Attempt to Explain to You What Happened with the Lion Tamer

He wasn't even a good lion tamer, not before you showed up.

He had always looked the part, with his whip and his chair and his spangled pants, but honestly, watching him in the cage with those lions was like watching a man stagger blindfolded across a four-lane highway. One night in Glens Falls, the chair slipped from his hand and the lions swatted it around the cage like a chew toy. In Council Bluffs, a claw snapped his patent-leather bandolier like an old shoestring. And in Granite City, a lion caught the whip between its jaws and yanked him around the ring like a fish on a line. It was a minor miracle every time he stepped out of the cage—bruised and bleeding, his outfit a web of sequins and crooked stitching. He didn't seem to care that the clapping was never the thunderous peal you'd expect when a man emerges from a cage full of wild animals, and he didn't care that it petered out before half a minute was up. He'd just stand there with his arms raised, like some avatar of victory, and he'd beam that ivory smile and shake his blond mane. You'd think the lions had just elected him king of the Serengeti.

THE FIRST TIME I saw you, I was alone behind the big top, adjusting the mix in the confetti buckets. Most of the others were still in bed, nursing hangovers or aching limbs, asking themselves for the ten thousandth time what it was going to take to get moving today.

Right away I knew you were no first-of-May, no circus rookie. Five-foot-nothing, barefoot in a leotard, you strutted up to me like you owned not just the big top but the fairgrounds it stood on, like the rest of us had better get your say-so before we turned a single somersault.

"So, you the new girl on the flying trapeze?" I said, although I knew without asking: you smelled like chalk dust and hairspray.

"What are you, some kind of clown?" you said, eyeing my tattered plaid pants and my flop-collared shirt, my white face and painted-on smile. I danced a little jig, letting my head loll from side to side, and ended with a pratfall—straight down on my keister.

Immediately I wished I hadn't done that.

Still, you smiled. It wasn't a toothy, whole-face-blooming-into-a-laugh sort of smile, but it was a smile. Then, without another word, you made tracks for the big top.

That confetti wasn't going to sort itself, but how could I take my eyes off you, with your legs like cables of braided silk? It wasn't just that you were beautiful; there are a lot of pretty ladies

in the circus, bearded and otherwise. It was that strut. I followed
you into the tent, and by the time my eyes adjusted to the light
filtering through the canvas, you were already halfway up the
ladder to the high wire. *Whoa-ho,* I said to myself, *a double threat:
The tightrope and the trapeze. The wire and the swing.*

The roustabouts had started to hoist the net into place, cursing
at the lines and jabbering about this broad who shows up out
of nowhere and puts them to work right in the middle of a
union-mandated pre-work coffee break. They were ornery that
morning, still grousing about the case of Jonah's luck they'd
had with the blow-off in Sandusky—the skies had opened, the
canvas became cement-heavy, and the fists of soaked rope that
gripped the tent pegs couldn't be pulled apart. Two days later
they were still looking for someone to piss on, and a greenhorn
tumbler was just the ticket.

"Hey down there," you said, your voice knifing through the
morning haze. "I don't want the net!"

They kept hoisting the lines because it's one thing to perform
without a net, but no one practices without one—unless you
want your first mistake to be your last. So this time you shouted,
"Gentlemen!" and that stopped them in their tracks, because no
one ever called them gentlemen. "I said no net!"

The net flopped to the floor of the big top, kicking up a fog
of sawdust. One of them called you a crazy bitch, but I swear the
words were tinged with respect and even a little awe.

You were at the top of the ladder, and although you could
have stepped lightly onto the tightrope, testing its thickness and
tension, you raised your arms above your head and cartwheeled

to the middle of the wire. I heard one of the razorbacks gasp. Another mumbled something that might have been a curse but could have been a prayer.

And me? My heart burst like a child's balloon. Right then and there I knew I loved you.

I MADE IT a habit to run into you on the midway whenever I scrounged for breakfast. There was always plenty of lukewarm coffee in the pie car, but tracking down a meal that didn't come with a side of day-old funnel cakes was a challenge.

In those early days I wasn't shy about giving advice: Watch out for the sword swallowers and the fire-eaters, I told you, because they were only interested in one thing. And steer clear of the midget couple, Tom and Tina Thumb. They had both cheated—him with the fat lady, her with the dog-faced boy—but they were as perfectly matched as salt and pepper shakers, and neither could call it quits. But here's something I don't remember, though I've squeezed my brain like a soggy dishrag: Did you ever ask me about him? Did I ever volunteer anything that made you think, *Why not?*

You didn't say much about yourself, and a lot of what you did tell me didn't add up. Once you said you had been born into the circus and another time that you'd run away and joined up when you were a little girl. You said your parents were your first audience and then later that they had never seen you perform. But the one thing you never wavered on was this: you had never worked with a net.

"It wouldn't count," you said one morning as we set up our

breakfast on the counter of the ring-toss booth. We'd looted bananas from dozing monkeys, apples left out for the Arabian stallions, honey from the trailer of the freak show's bee man. "It just wouldn't, if you knew you could fall and get right back up, like nothing had happened."

"What if you're trying something new?" I said. "You know, in practice."

You smirked. "You either know what you're doing or you don't."

I tried to tell you that I knew exactly what you were talking about—that you and I were like two sides of the same coin, even if one side was engraved with the face of some mythic diva and the reverse with the dull, muddy squiggle of a horse's ass. Still, I knew that when I went out there every night, the only options were mass murder or a public hanging. Either I killed or I bombed. I don't think you got it, though—then or ever—because in your eyes, you were risking the long fall from the top of the tent, and I was just another groundling hoofing it around the center ring. Come to think of it, I don't think you ever really appreciated what the rest of us did. We were just the scenery: the human cannonballs with their nightly blowups, the elephant riders preening like royalty while their pachyderms did the heavy lifting, and the clowns, sweating and grinding for every laugh, our stomachs in knots for fear that this might be the night when nobody laughed and we'd stand out there naked, wilting under the glare of a thousand cut-the-crap stares. Or maybe that's just me.

Looking back, I don't know what I was expecting—okay,

I do, but I was smart enough to know that it wasn't going to happen without a bop on the head, a bad case of amnesia, and a tropical island where no one could remind you who you really were.

Then came that first night—your big debut.

I should have known something was up when the lion tamer strode out of the cage in better shape than usual. No stitches required. The applause from the local gillies wasn't exactly hearty, but it seemed a little more genuine. Then, as the lights cut out on him, a single spotlight lasered on the ringmaster, who directed the crowd's attention to the uppermost reaches of the tent, where you were frozen in place, the trapeze in your hands. "Ladies and gentlemen! I present to you the aerialist, who dances on the high wire and works magic on the trapeze. The flying girl, the acrobat of the air. Thrill to her death-defying feats! Gape in amazement as she flirts with death, because, folks—hold on to your hats—there's nothing between her and the floor but the force of gravity! That's right, she does it all without a net!" I swear the sides of the tent snapped like a ship's sail as the crowd, in one big gasp, sucked the free air out of the big top.

You soared. Head over heels—once, twice, a third time—a hundred feet above the floor. There wasn't a sound among the yokels who packed the bleachers, their necks craned upward, their eyes following the klieg lights. Every time that your body snapped open like a switchblade, your sequined leotard burst into a thousand tiny flashbulbs. When you came out of a rotation, arms extended, there wasn't a single heart beating. You twirled and floated, riding on the fear and wonder of the crowd, and when you finally came to rest on the platform, they absolutely exploded.

The applause lasted for hours, or so it seemed, but eventually the crowd grew peckish for some new treat. While their eyes were drawn to a family of Canadian acrobats, I waited near the bottom of the ladder to congratulate you—and, if the opportunity arose, to pour my heart into your hands. I counted down the dwindling number of rungs (yes, the view was exquisite, and from the tips of my size 24 shoes to the top of my busted stovepipe hat, I wanted you), but before your feet touched the floor, the lion tamer had you in his arms. He crushed you up against his chest—I'll admit it, the guy was ripped—and you buried your hands in his thick pile of hair. Then you kissed him.

You had not mentioned this over breakfast.

IT WAS AFTER that kiss that I decided to start performing that new bit, the takeoff on the lion tamer's act, where I used Scottie terriers with tutus around their necks for lions. I'd fill my back pockets with kibble so the terriers would chase me in circles trying to tear the seat out of my pants, and by the end of the bit, my clothes would be shredded, my tiny chair broken to pieces, and I'd have two or three dogs hanging on to my padded rear. I'd been holding off, because I really didn't know how the lion tamer would take it—just a joke, right? All in good fun. But after I saw him in a clinch with you, I didn't care.

That's not true. I cared. I wanted the laughter of the crowd to drown him; all the laughs that the crowd held back when he was in the cage would come pouring out when they saw me. Not just because the bit was funny, but because the crowd would see that I was goofing on him, and I'd get my laughs and the ones they were too polite or too scared to uncork on him. But it was just for laughs. Honestly. That's all I wanted.

The dog-tamer act was a big hit, but the joke was on me. I planned to go on with it right after the lion tamer's act. Bing-bang. Agony, then ecstatic laughter. The problem was, he was great that night; everything a lion tamer is supposed to be. Forceful. Authoritative. Daring. For once, he lived up to the words of the ringmaster's nightly, and heretofore ironic, introduction: the Man with the Indomitable Will. He cracked his whip and thrust the chair and I couldn't tell who was more surprised, me or the lions. He shouted commands and the lions obeyed. Nothing too technically difficult—jumping through hoops, sitting up on their hind legs—but he pulled it off without a hitch. He even finished by prying open a lion's mouth and sticking that big blond head of his between the cat's jaws. I thought for sure the lion was going to snatch his head off like a grape from a vine, but the big cat didn't even twitch. If a lion can think, I know exactly what was on its mind: *Who* is *this guy?* I kept asking myself the same question.

He finished to robust applause. I wouldn't say *thunderous,* but the crowd was impressed. And then it was my turn—me with a new costume modeled on his crisscross sequined bandoliers drooping into my baggy pants. The Scotties did their part, and the audience laughed in all the right places. Laughed a lot, actually. It was a great bit, but it had none of its intended punch. It was supposed to be two parts funny mixed with one part catharsis, spiked with a shot of derision. A satire. Or a parody—one or the other. What do I know? I'm no clown-college clown, but that's what I was aiming for. But now that he had his act together, I was the only one worth laughing at. Which is my job—I'm the one they're supposed to be laughing at—but still.

After a week of asserting his newfound mastery of all things vicious and feline, the lion tamer became unbearable. When he was one misstep away from being lion chow, it was easy to work up some sympathy for him—or it would have been if I weren't congenitally deficient in the sympathy department. But now? It was bad enough that he was in the spotlight, in the center ring, and had you in his life. Now he seemed to think he deserved the attention. Maybe I was the only one who noticed it, but he was acting like he, with his buff arms and bushy mane, was the only one who belonged under the big top.

Here I go again, yakking like a sideshow barker, but I have to wonder: This high-and-mighty king-of-the-jungle routine didn't bother you? I've tried to convince myself that you couldn't help it, because let me tell you, some women are just drawn to lion tamers. It must be the smell of the lions—some pheromone that women can't resist. I don't know if he told you this, but even when he wasn't impressing *anyone* with his ability to bend the lions to his indomitable will, he was still getting laid like a sailor on leave. He used to talk about it all the time, and he had this way of making it sound like it was such a chore, telling me how women expect a lot from a lion tamer. In the sack, he meant. They would growl at him and curl their fingers into claws and bare their teeth. More than once, a woman asked him to use his whip or prod her with an overturned chair. And the women who brought the lion tamer back to their apartments always wanted to see his scars. They wanted to hear the stories behind each mark and kiss the ropy flesh and say, *There, now; all better.*

"You clowns have it easy," he once said. "All you have to do is make them laugh." I swear, I almost popped him one, right in the kisser. And not with a cream pie.

Do you remember the time you told me he needed a better moniker? It was late one afternoon as we packed for the trek to the next town. We'd had a good run through Kalamazoo, Crown Point, and the Quad Cities, but it was time to move on. You said he needed a name that looked good on a poster—an all-caps red-letter sobriquet.

I was wrapping up bottles of seltzer, stacking pie plates, stowing the balloon-animal balloons. "How about 'the Preposterous'?"

You cracked a smile—yes, you did—before you said, "I was thinking 'the Great' or 'the Magnificent,' but those seem—"

"Incongruous?"

"No," you said, the smile blooming into something larger, "too common. Everyone thinks they're great or amazing or magnificent. It needs to be"—and here you paused—"more . . . awesome." You cocked your head, perhaps considering a thesaurus full of possibilities. "Hey, what about that?"

" 'The Awful'?" I said. "Sure. It's kinda catchy. It suits him."

"For someone who calls himself a clown, you're not as funny as you think you are." That's what you said—trust me, I have this committed to memory—but at the same time, your smile hadn't faded. Can't you see what this meant to me? A smile. A chuckle. A stifled laugh. To me, these have all the come-hither power of a wink, a pout, a gaze that lasts a second too long.

And what about the time you told me he needed a new costume? "Maybe something in an animal print," you said. The image of the lion tamer in leopard-spotted jodhpurs flared into my mind: Ridiculous and horrifying all at once. A getup like that could put my dog-tamer bit out of business; another case of life overtaking art.

"Now, that," I said, "would be awesome."

You let loose with a big laugh and I should have been in my glory. Score one for me, and a goose egg for the lion tamer. But I was beginning to see that he had been right: getting a laugh was the easy part.

The funny thing was, you were burning up mental energy on how best to describe his greatness when all along you were the only thing awesome about that circus. Take it from me, who was nothing more than a tiny, red-nosed planet in a far-flung orbit—you were the star, and you knew it. You had to. After that first night, crowds packed the stands in town after town, waiting for your act. You did things in the upper reaches of the big top that were impossible even in a dream. Some people looked up and thought: *Brave. Magical. Intoxicating.* You were living a life they were too timid to even contemplate. Others saw you use the trapeze like a catapult and the tightrope like a dance floor, and then they looked at the empty space where the net was supposed to be, and they thought: *Naive. Foolish. Shameless.* But they watched, just as spellbound as the others, waiting—and, I have to wonder, hoping—for you to get what you deserved. Depending on who you asked, either you loved life more than the rest of us or you craved death and you spent every night auditioning a new crowd of witnesses.

Maybe that second group, the nasty naysayers, saw something that I didn't see then but see now: All that time you were up there, you weren't flying—you were falling. You dressed it up, with the flipping and the spinning and the soaring, but from the second you let go of that trapeze, you were plummeting to the unforgiving floor.

And maybe that's why none of your catchers lasted more than a week. They were close enough to see what was what. And you sure didn't make it easy on them. In every trapeze act that I've ever seen, the tumblers take turns: one night you've got your legs wrapped tight around the trapeze as you wait to catch your partner; the next you're the one counting on your partner to be there when you come out of a tuck and stick out your hands. But you were the only one who flew, and the weight of it—night after night without a net—got to be too much for them. It never seemed to bother you; if anything, it inspired you. Like I've said, you soared—or appeared to, which was good enough for everyone under the big top. But the guys waiting to reel you in—guys whose names we never bothered to learn—were worn out, used up, exhausted. And while they always caught you, they could only do it for so long. The poor, lucky saps.

WAS IT THESE small moments—packing for the next town, shooting the breeze, watching you tumble—that pushed me to say what I said? Of course it was, but it was bigger than just that. It was the whole way we lived—in trailers and tents like gypsies, like refugees, like some kind of traveling circus. The romantically inclined probably think we're one big carefree troupe, laughing and drinking and dancing the mazurka, but romance here is as rare as an honest answer. There are no harlequin tents, no barrel-roofed gypsy wagons. Our trailers are frosted with rust. Our pitted windows spill fluorescent light onto the hardpacked fairgrounds and blacktopped lots. The tents are drafty or else stifling. From inside come shouts or sobs or the rare soft words that only fill our hearts with envy at another's happiness or hasty climax. The only advantage of our portable habitations is that we can cluster and recluster them depending on the latest feuds or fondnesses, the couplings and the coming-aparts.

This is a roundabout way of saying that one night I heard noises from his trailer—thumps, bangs, the echoes of exertion—and I thought, *Here we go again.* Another night torturing myself with images of you and him: your teeth bared, your back arched in feline submission, your throat emitting a low rumble. (Please tell me, if nothing else, that you weren't one of those women.) But before I could stuff my fingers in my ears, it became clear that you were griping, not groaning. After weeks when I swore I could hear every whispered moment, I strained and stretched but couldn't make out a word. What filtered through the tin-can walls of his trailer were the smoky remnants of anger and frustration.

I confess I went to bed happy. I think that's the name for what I was feeling; I've never been good with names. I only knew I hadn't felt it in a long time, and it made me giddy to lie there in my sheets and think that I might have stirred something up by putting in my time and playing games with monikers and sobriquets. I had stalked around the edges of the thing I most wanted to say, and look what had happened: A rift had opened. Perhaps even a door that I could walk through. And while I was in the business of wishful thinking, I put in a request that I would have one clean shot at the bop on the head, the island, and all the rest.

THEN THERE WAS that night, in that town. I don't remember where—let's just say it was somewhere in the heartland; we spent a lot of time in the heartland. We were walking the midway and you were telling me how hard things were for him, with the big cats lunging and the crowd hungry for excitement. But your heart wasn't in it. You were telling me this because you always told me this.

You shrugged and said that his father was a lion tamer, and his mother was a lion tamer's assistant. So what choice did he have?

"I don't know," I said. "My old man was no clown, but maybe that skips a generation."

"Seriously," you said. "What else was he supposed to do?"

"How about being a traveling salesman? An electrical engineer? Auto-parts dealer?"

"If only it were that easy," you said. "We'd all be traveling salesmen, right?"

We stopped near the booth where the swami read palms. I felt boldness, never one of my strong suits, rising inside me, buoyed by the memory of that happiness I'd felt in the darkness of my trailer. "No, we wouldn't," I said. "You'd still be you and I'd still be me—but he could be someone else entirely."

Your eyes had a dreamy, faraway look to them. If he were someone else entirely, would you have been more interested in him or less? If you were someone else entirely, could that person see herself with me? If I were someone else—but that's enough of that. All of these thoughts were spinning through my noggin, but what was I supposed to do with them? Or with you?

That was when the words popped out of me: "Why do you do this?" I meant everything: the trapeze, the wire, the lion tamer, the time you spent with me, the empty space where the net should be. I left it up to you to decide how much of the question you wanted to bite off.

"I guess I like it," you said, which cleared up nothing.

"You guess?"

"I must, right? Why else would I do it?" Whether you were asking a question or defending yourself, I didn't know. All I knew was that your eyes were on me, and the temperature out there on the midway had skyrocketed. Had it ever been so hot under the spotlights, in the tent in midsummer with the thousands sweating in their seats and the trampled straw and pissed-on sawdust rising, rising, rising through my head? Better men than me would have had an answer for you, or at least something to say. I had nothing. You were staring right at me, but your eyes were fixed on some secret spot inside you. If that door had been left open, it seemed to me that the wind was pushing it shut.

"Say something funny," you said.

"I love you" tumbled out of me. The words pushed into the open air like clowns from a car.

Your eyes snapped shut like I'd slapped you. "That's not funny."

And you were right. It wasn't funny—it was hilarious. Coming from me, it was absolutely ridiculous.

As time crawled from one second to the next, your head ticked from side to side in a slow-motion *no,* and I could feel the pressure of all of the things I'd left unsaid building in my brain. If I had been a cartoon, steam would have shot from my ears. I would have blown my stack, complete with a red whistle and wisps of smoke pouring from my smoldering dome. But I am what I am, and I did what clowns do. I started turning my arm faster and faster, as if cranking some giant flywheel, and when I couldn't go any faster I ratcheted my fist up and bopped myself smack on the top of the head. It's a standard sight gag—anyone who's been to a circus once has seen it a million times—and it's supposed to end with a woozy roll of the eyes, a loll of the tongue, and, after a second's delay, a gimpy-kneed collapse. But I left all of that out. I wasn't going for the gag. I wanted so badly to believe that my arm had become a sledgehammer that could drive my body deep into the ground, deeper than the pegs that keep the big top tight, deep enough to get away from you and the truth of what I'd said, and the truth of what you felt.

THIS IS HOW what happened happened: I heard you behind the cotton-candy stand, and I honestly thought you were talking to me. I didn't so much hear your voice as detect a fluttering in the atmosphere. It was a whisper, an intake of breath, nothing more. I heard it again, then again, growing louder as I drew near.

There were hay bales piled in the gap between the booth and the outer wall of the big top, and as I poked my head over the top of one of the bales, my nose rising like a poster-paint sun, I saw it all. It wasn't me you were talking to, and it wasn't the lion tamer either. And it wasn't me straddling you, and it wasn't the corrugated expanse of my back concealing everything but your sculpted legs and taped feet.

Ladies and gentlemen, in the center ring, I give you the strongman, the human steam engine! Watch as he twists bars of solid iron like saltwater taffy! Thrill to the display of brute force as he juggles bank safes like baseballs! Nothing is beyond his power, and nothing can crush his forged-steel frame!

My knees buckled, and in that moment of ecstasy (yours, of course) and agony (mine, as always), I swear I heard you laugh, a tinkling sound like a bag full of broken glass, like some candy-faced kid pounding the twinkly end of a piano.

As I staggered away from the hay bales, the water-squirting daisy in my lapel started gushing and my shoes flapped against the flattened earth. That laughter followed me, echoing, rising in my head, louder than any tent full of yokels in any town I'd ever played. It broke over me like a tidal wave, and that's when I stumbled out onto the midway and ran right into him.

I want to make this part clear. I didn't go looking for him. I didn't have a tale to tell. I tripped, I fell, I looked up. And there he was.

He looked golden. Since his act had taken off, he had acquired a deeply bronze tan—a sheen, even—which only made him seem more like the lord of some grassland kingdom. He peered down, and before he said a word, he shook that mane of his. I wouldn't have been surprised if he had roared at me. But instead, he asked a simple question: Did I know where you were? I was practically deaf from the laughter ringing in my head, and there he was, so polished, so confident, so unshakable. Without getting up, without dusting off my pants, without saying a word, I pointed one white-gloved hand down the path that led to the hay bales behind the cotton-candy booth.

I WOULD HAVE explained all of this if you had let me. All I knew was what I heard around the midway: You were spending all of your time up on the wire, the lion tamer was holed up with his big cats, and the strongman had already been seen testing his mettle with the tattooed lady. The lion tamer claimed he was putting the finishing touches on a brand-new act, something no one had ever seen before. In the meantime he was still doing the old routine, but he was slipping. And here's the part that really got me: It wasn't any fun to watch. Before, he had been oblivious, like a dopey kid trying to jam a fork into an electrical outlet. You had to admire his moxie, even if you knew he was in for a shock. Now he was just plain angry, whipping the cats through their paces. After watching this for two nights and a matinee, I put my dog-tamer bit on hiatus. He wasn't bad enough for it to be funny the way I wanted, and he wasn't good enough for it to be funny the way the ringmaster wanted. We figured we'd muddle through with something else until his new act was ready, and then we'd bring back the Scotties. The crowd loved those Scotties.

Then, the grand finale. The night the lion tamer was going to unveil his new act, and the night I would debut a bigger and better dog-tamer bit. I wanted to hold off until I knew which way things were going to break with the lion tamer, but the ringmaster insisted. He could tell how tense things had been around the big top, and he believed that one good show could clear it all up.

From the first minutes after the come-in, as the rubes lined up and handed over their ducats, there was a buzz in the air. It continued to build right up until the lights went down and the big top was bathed in black. When the spotlights came back up, the lion tamer was in the center ring, surrounded by his big cats. Only it wasn't just his big cats. It was a pride of them. He must have had a dozen lions in there. Torches guttered at every corner of the cage, and an entire row of flaming hoops was fanned out across the middle. The lions looked skittish, distracted by the spotlights, angered by all that fire, sniping at one another and feeling decidedly unbent by the until-recently indomitable will of the lion tamer. Who, by the way, looked awful. Like he hadn't slept in days, hadn't showered, hadn't been near a blow-dryer. Even at his worst, he had always had his vanity to keep him afloat.

I don't know what he had planned. It's a safe bet that he wanted to run the entire line of big cats through that fiery tunnel, just to prove that he could do it—and it might have really been something to see. When he waded in among the lions, the crowd went church-quiet. He started shouting, urging the lions in one direction or another, and when they didn't respond, he went to the whip. He waved it over his head like a pompom, and the lions seemed happy to ignore him until he jerked it back in one quick motion and the tip of the whip bit into the haunches of the biggest of the cats in that cage.

The lion's yellow eyes narrowed, and then it pounced. No growling, no swatting, no warning. It pushed off with its meaty legs and before he could raise his little chair, it was on top of him. Once he was on the ground, the other lions moved in.

The lights went out in the center ring—too late, I'm afraid, to spare the ladies and gentlemen and children of all ages a firelit sight that would linger long after we left town. And that's when the lights came on over me and the dogs, because that's how it works in the circus. When something goes wrong, you send in the clowns. So the lights came on and we snapped to life, the dogs with their tutu manes and me in my spangled bandoliers and my pockets full of kibble.

The crowd was distracted for a second or two—I am the shiny penny on the sidewalk, the lightbulb that flares before it dies—but once people caught the gist of the act, they turned on me as surely as the big cats had turned on the lion tamer. Garbage rained down on me, and I swear it wasn't until the first wadded-up bag of popcorn hit me in my big ugly mug that I realized how the dog-tamer bit must have looked. But what was I supposed to do, pick up the Scotties and juggle them? I had one act ready to go. That's all I had.

I froze out there, and the second I stopped moving, the Scotties dug their teeth into the seat of my pants with all their little terrier jaws could give. This indignity, not thirty feet from what was left of the lion tamer, sent the crowd into a cascade of boos—booing like I had never heard before. In a word: *thunderous*. And while the crowd pelted me with paper cups and half-eaten hot dogs, I looked up into the big top and saw you on the platform, sparkling vaguely in the shadows. You had seen it all; you would understand that I was only doing my job. I tried to use my own will, which no one had ever described as indomitable, to draw your eyes off the darkened cage and over to me. I wanted you to see how I had been swept up in all of this and to give me one sequined smile, one dewy look from those kohl-black eyes. There I was, the focus of the crowd's anger and disgust, but not for one second did I blame you for any of it, not for choosing the lion tamer, or burying your fingernails in the strongman's beefy back, or even for my own predicament: the dogs, the boos, my ass. I could have laid this at your petite, rope-burned feet, but I didn't—I couldn't—because all of this mess and misery connected me to you.

You could have looked at me, and all of this would have been clear. Instead, you stood on that shaky cocktail table of a platform, feeling gravity's pull. Below you lay the horror of the lion cage, the fury of the crowd, and one clownish heart calling out for a moment's tender notice. Which of these caused you to do what you did? Which one of us—the strong and weak, brave and cowardly, funny and foolish—steeled you for that first step? No lights lit your way, but in the darkness you walked onto that wire like it could take you out of the big top and away from all of us.

Acknowledgments

Thanks to my agent, Gail Hochman, my editor, Ben George, and Maggie Southard Gladstone and the team at Little, Brown who helped to bring this book into the world.

To Chris Tilghman, Deborah Eisenberg, Ann Beattie, and my friends in the University of Virginia MFA program whose generosity and support came when I needed it most. To my teachers at the University of North Carolina at Chapel Hill, especially Jill McCorkle—and in loving memory of Doris Betts, Max Steele, and Robert Kirkpatrick.

To Heidi Pitlor, an early champion. To every reader of the slush pile who ever moved one of my stories up the line, and to every magazine editor who ever said yes.

To my own traveling circus and the life of thrills, spills, and laughter they bring: Nora, Fiona, Cormac, and Greta. And always to Margaret—expert juggler, wire walker, ringmaster, and tamer of ferocious beasts.

About the Author

Brendan Mathews is the author of the novel *The World of Tomorrow*, which was long-listed for the Center for Fiction First Novel Prize. His stories have twice appeared in *The Best American Short Stories* and in *Glimmer Train, Virginia Quarterly Review, Southern Review,* and other publications. A former Fulbright Scholar to Ireland, he lives with his family in Lenox, Massachusetts, and teaches at Bard College at Simon's Rock.